Open Strings

Gordon Simms

LEAF BY LEAF

Published by Leaf by Leaf
an imprint of Cinnamon Press,
Office 49019, PO Box 15113, Birmingham, B2 2NJ
www.cinnamonpress.com

The right of Gordon Simms to be identified as author of this work
has been asserted by him in accordance with the Copyright,
Designs and Patent Act, 1988. © 2023, Gordon Simms.
Print Edition ISBN 978-1-78864-973-5
British Library Cataloguing in Publication Data. A CIP record for
this book can be obtained from the British Library.

Designed and typeset in Adobe Caslon by Cinnamon Press.
Cover design by Adam Craig from original artwork by colin ross jack,
used with kind permission.
Cinnamon Press is represented by Inpress.

Praise for *Open Strings*

Open Strings captures so well the rough edges, sharp corners, loose ends, terrors and daily miracles of childhood; its rivalries and moments of unexpected tenderness. A compelling, first-rate story that invites the reader to become a participant and a collaborator; thereby drawing the reader into a debate on the power of story, of memory and on the nature of 'reality' itself.

Jackie Fellague, poet and environmentalist

I felt I was stepping into a bygone age. Beautiful writing, evocative yet with a poetic economy of style. The quirky characters and the landscape are deliciously encapsulated. So much to dwell on: a wonderful novella.

Emma Curtis, novelist

A vivid picture of a bygone era, brilliantly brought to life through detailed observation. The reader is effortlessly and intimately involved in the narrative.

Bernard Lord, poet

Gordon Simms captures the spirit of a rural, post-war childhood in this enchanting story. Through his evocative descriptions and masterful dialogue we see how one boy's friendships and rivalries prepare him for the wider world.

Harriet Springbett, author

Acknowledgements

of the founder members of the Writers' Block, way back when, whose inspirational experimentation gave rise to the beginning of this book.

And to Jan and the team at Cinnamon Press for their help in completing it.

Author biography

Gordon Simms trained as an English and Drama teacher, Gordon lectured at Rose Bruford College of Speech and Drama before becoming a Drama Advisor and Head of Performing Arts. He is the author of several plays, including the prize-winning *Stop Press*. His ten-minute play *Zero Contract* was performed in 2017 in France where he has organised three bilingual literary festivals. He ran Segora International writing competitions for fifteen years, celebrating winning entries with readings, book launches and workshops. He has judged poetry, playwriting and short story competitions. A prolific poet, he has been successful in over ninety competitions and widely anthologised. His collection *Uphill to the Sea* won the Biscuit Prize in 2011. His short fiction has been published in *The Real Jazz Baby* and shortlisted for *Fish*. He has broadcast with the BBC and read at various venues in England, Scotland, Ireland and France.

to Jocelyn
for her constant support and encouragement

I will revise,
rewind, fast-forward, edit.
I capture their antic play that I might say
That must have been last summer or
Yes, that was my childhood – there!

(from *Uphill to the Sea*)

Open Strings

FLOOD

Of all the stories flowing through my childhood, this is the one I remember. I remember the flavour of it, its smells, the feel and finally, worst of all, the taste of it. Sometimes I requested it, and sometimes it rolled in on some kind of moon-driven rotation. It was called The Flood. Or, if it wasn't, it should have been, because that's what it was about, and the terrible impression it left was of a world deep in water. And if any of you doubt the power of story you'd better stop listening, now. (I say 'listening' because you often hear a voice in your head when reading). So haunting was this story, my first dream would be The Flood dream. Hours later when I woke that would be the only dream I saw. The Flood.

Usually the dream was worse than the story because the story came to an end and the book would be closed and the light would go out and with it my mother. I couldn't listen if my father read it. I would wrap the pillow round my ears. Once I buried my head under the bolster. After that he must have decided I couldn't stand the sound of his voice. From then on, he talked about me, rather than to me. I could hear him then all right.

"That boy had better come to his senses." Or "It's time he woke his ideas up."

One night I must have been falling asleep before my mother finished the story. I took the book carefully, for it was like one of the afflictions in the Old Testament, and said goodnight and she switched off the main light and left the room. Perhaps she went downstairs to finish the washing-up. I don't know: I'm guessing. I imagine her hands sloshing about in the lather, the glistening plates and pans on the draining board, the smell of wet wood, the drip, drip of the water trickling from the runnels and falling into clear circles in the soapy froth of the sink.

I gingerly held the book and looked at the cover. The Flood, it said. I suppose I'm imagining that, but that's the title I see. Of course, I could read by then. So why was it read to me? Perhaps I demanded it, once in a while, for a change. Perhaps it was the only way I could address that story, never daring to read it for myself. Possibly, now and again, it was considered a good thing that I should be terrified.

We have a fascination for things we least like. We're drawn to the bottom of the garden to again see the dead blackbird we discovered earlier. We lift the plank of wood to peer at the writhing worms. We go to the water's edge and imagine ourselves falling, the water rising.

Twilight: the boy and the girl and their pet collie being washed away downstream on an upturned table. The upper branches of trees poking through the eddies. The roofs of cottages, their thatch returning to whence it came. Biblical stuff, isn't it? But no Saviour, no angel, no firemen or coastguards in solid launches. Just the blue of the dress, the brown shirt and grey trousers, the indigo sky and black water—except for the white swirl breaking over the front of the table.

I gazed a long time at the cover. Dots and speckles appeared, so that the water took on movement and the table seemed to float. Then my head dropped. I jerked open my eyes and ran the first two fingers of my right hand along the edge of the cover. My father had taught me always to go to the top right-hand corner, because of his theory. I used to listen to his theories before I was unable to bear his voice, and I used to take notice of them. Perhaps that's the real reason I stopped listening to him. This theory concerned the way people handled books. He said they rested them on their laps and were careless turning the pages. They would either push the page into a fold like a wave and risk creasing it, or turn the bottom right-hand corner up, making it dog-eared.

That's why I remember the bit about the collie. Perhaps the illustrator wanted to give the idea that the faithful pet would somehow guard the children and take them to safety. But there was no bank or island, only what, in the distance, might have been the horizon, almost indistinct from the sky.

I slid my index finger under the lip of the cover and opened the book. I read the publisher's address and the names of the author and the artist who had painted the collie. I can't remember any of that now. Then I turned to the first page of the story proper.

The first paragraph was about clouds gathering until

they filled the sky. It was gloomy, and there was silence in the countryside, as if the world was waiting. As I reached the end, where the birds had stopped singing, I realised I'd cut my finger. You can do that on paper. I expect you've done it sometimes. I had that thin, sharp feeling, only when I looked it wasn't bleeding, so I was wrong. I couldn't even see one of those tiny marks that graze the skin without really cutting it, though the lamp wasn't very bright so I might not have seen it anyway. But I could feel it.

The second paragraph was about a great wind that blew in from the ocean. I knew from the cover that there was an ocean, but I didn't know how far away it was when the story started. This wind swept the clouds into heaps, not letting sunlight through. I didn't need to turn back to the cover to see that sky. As I neared the end of that paragraph, I ran my fingers to the top edge of the page, just as I'd been taught. I finished the paragraph and curled my finger under the single sheet of paper. It was then I saw a smudge. The stem of a *t* had stretched to the edge of the page, tracing the route my finger must have taken. The cross of the *t* had become a branch, so the letter looked like a tree, leaning as if it was being uprooted. On the line above, an *o* and what might have been an *l* had blurred. The *o* had filled in like the sky, and lost some of its roundness. The *l* had lengthened, splashing at the bottom like a waterfall. They were next to each other in the same word (it might have been cloud, mightn't it?) which looked larger than it should have done. Nearby was an *h*, like a dripping tap.

Making a mess of a book got you into serious trouble in our house. Books were precious, a kind of magic—that was another theory. A dirty thumbprint got you a telling off: spilling, tearing or crumpling got a good thrashing. Thrashings never felt good to me, but then I never handed one out. I wonder if I liked books in the first place because they were dangerous.

The blurred area was grey, where the rest of the page was cream. As I watched, it spread, like the cloud. I thought I'd better turn the page so I couldn't see it. If I did that, shut my eyes, and counted to ten, it might go away. I also got the idea that if I turned the page quickly the movement would dry it, like wind through the weekly wash. I knew about friction, you see. It was a silly idea, but I was getting desperate. I suppose that's why I can remember it, because I was so anxious. You do recall tiny little details when you're in shock, and I suppose I was in a kind of shock. I also remember hoping by the time the book was picked up by anyone else, all sign of the blur would have vanished.

The idea came and went in a flash, like a raindrop. You don't remember single raindrops, you're thinking. But you do, you know. I bet every one of you can remember a particular raindrop that fell close to you at some time in your life, even years ago. You just think about it. It might have landed on your arm, or made a dark patch on the road in front of you. You might have heard it on the earth, or maybe on a tin roof or skylight, even if at first you didn't realise it was rain. And if it was a hot day, you'd have smelt it—that warm, treacly smell from tarmac or the sweetness given off by a leaf.

Well, I tried it. I whipped the page over as smartly as I could. The word I had been looking at, that may have been cloud, had come through and was lying back to front and inside out, where it shouldn't have been at all.

I closed the book. The cover felt damp. I opened my eyes as wide as I could and blinked several times. I opened the book. The introductory page with the names on and the first two pages of the story had stuck together. On Page Three the black letters were blurring one after another. Some grew very large, then dwindled, swaying like waterweed below the surface. I slammed the book shut. A drop of water squeezed out: the beginning of The Flood.

I'm a Scorpio. November. They play the national anthem on my birthday, but not for me. Scorpio is a water sign. I expect you know that. I didn't, not at first. People are sometimes afraid of Scorpios. They're nothing like as afraid as Scorpios are of themselves though, believe me.

When the book began to drip, I was petrified. I couldn't move a muscle for at least half a minute. That might not sound long, but you just try it. Sit there for thirty seconds without moving, with your eyes and mouth wide open—as if you're screaming. Don't scream though, I can't stand it. Start now.

The trouble is with your face fixed like that you probably can't see when thirty seconds are up, and I don't want you counting them silently to yourself because that would give you something to think about, and there wasn't a thought in my head. When people say they're not thinking about anything, they don't mean that literally. You realise that, I'm sure. It's actually impossible to think about nothing. Experts don't agree on how we dream, so you might be thinking even when asleep. You've had a good thirty seconds, by the way.

What did it feel like, doing and trying to think of nothing? Difficult, isn't it? After all, nothing is an idea of some sort. You've got to be in a pretty severe state of something or other to think about nothing, even for that short time.

When I came back to my senses, water was trickling from the book. The bedcover was damp, and that would mean trouble and some embarrassing questions. I had to stop this flow. I clutched the book: when I squeezed it, however, the water came faster.

It took a long time to dawn on me what's probably obvious to you by now. All I had to do was get the window open. I pulled my legs from under the bedclothes, cradling the book with my arms stretched in front. Really, I should have used one hand on the catch, but I had been brought up so strictly in the matter of caring for books that even now I had to hold The Flood with both hands. I managed to hook my toe round the bedside chair. I dragged it across the lino—I was a bit worried about the noise, but if I'd known what was to come, I wouldn't have bothered about that one bit. I stood on the chair, keeping the book level. I needed to get my elbow under the catch without spilling. Water ran up my sleeves, but I didn't let that stop me. What did hold me up was the catch itself. It had always been hard to open. Usually I gripped it really tightly with both hands to make it work. I couldn't get enough leverage on it with an elbow, especially as, with the book, I couldn't give it a good upward thump.

I made a last effort to lift the catch. The book slithered from my hands and splashed onto the floor. A jet of water hit me under the chin. I slewed sideways and lost balance. I fell on the book, which shot away and spewed over the wall above my bed. The lamp went out with a bang.

I stood; my bare feet submerged. Had I concentrated on the window things might still not have turned out so badly, but I was intent on finding the book to smother the fountain issuing from it. I was paddling in inches of water. I couldn't tell where the book was. Was it floating, submerged, or trapped behind furniture? For all I knew it could have flown to the top of the wardrobe, or, for that matter, dissolved.

I splashed about frantically. I couldn't worry about noise now. Something bumped me in the back. I reached behind to discover the chair, floating waist high. I panicked. I forgot about the window, which opened onto a sloping roof the cat used to climb, and down which I might have slithered to safety. I waded to where the door should be. I found the handle, just below the surface. It was slippery, but I managed to turn it. I knew how much to twist it by its feel because (as you have, I dare say) I'd often crept out of my room in the dark when I couldn't sleep to walk silently about the house.

The handle turned as expected, but when I tried to pull nothing happened. I tried harder, but I was floundering in chest-high water whose weight exceeded any power I could generate. You hear a lot about that sort of thing in Physics. I wouldn't recommend finding out about it the way I did. I banged on the door and shouted, several times. My voice rose to a wail. That's why I said I can't stand screaming: it reminds me of what it sounded like to me, in my head, in my room, in my Flood, in which I was shortly to drown.

If you've heard anything of this kind before, this is where you'd probably expect to be told that I woke and was mightily relieved to discover it was only a dream. Well, a nightmare then. I'm sorry I can't tell you that because I was already awake, and it was all too real. Come on, you're thinking, you can't expect us to believe that! You'll see.

I felt someone pushing from the other side. The door was opening. There was a gasp and a surge of water, and I was flushed out on to the landing. If you've seen one of those weirs fashioned out of stone steps, you'll know how the river rushes down them, spilling white, black and brown in a torrent. Our staircase must have looked like that, only with myself and bits and pieces of bedroom furniture plunging down it. The front door would stop me, I thought, but it had already been wrenched from its hinges, and I was carried into the garden. I could see only the wispy tops of the taller trees beyond the shrubbery, and I was brushed past them in seconds.

Now although I'm a Scorpio, as I told you, I hate water. I was always too frightened to be able to swim. I could never relax, and had no coordination. I would thrash around, staying afloat until my energy failed, when I would sink. So you'll realise I'd no chance of saving myself in this phenomenal inundation except by clambering on to a cottage roof or clutching a topmost branch of one of the ash trees that lined the road. But they weren't near enough, and their dim shapes rushed past. I think I nearly lost consciousness through exhaustion and cold fear. But then I heard a dog barking. I saw Prince, my grandfather's Labrador on whose back I once rode when a toddler. I'd often been told about that; I couldn't remember it. But sometimes when you hear about an event from your earliest years, you make a picture in your mind of what it must have looked like, and before long it's as vivid as a memory, so you can't tell the difference.

I don't know what he was doing there. I'm sure he'd died some years before, not long after he'd given me that ride around the yard. And before you pick me up on it, he was a Labrador, not a collie. I expect you've noticed when illustrations in a book disappoint you. They show things that don't look as you've imagined from reading the story. A few pages into the book you come across a picture you didn't know was there (otherwise you'd have looked at it first): it might be of one of the main characters, and it's irritating if it doesn't seem like the person you've pictured. Worse, sometimes the artist has missed something important, painting the wrong colour hair or different clothes, something that contradicts what's been written.

I'm saying all this because, in the gloom, I could see

it was Prince, and that he was sitting on the missing front door, using it as a raft. It was his bark all right. I recognised it straight away, and I can tell you I was relieved to hear it. If he had been painted, I was glad a mistake had been made, because the only collie I knew in the village was a grumpy animal that snarled at me whenever I passed its gate.

There was a white wave over the front of the raft, just as pictured on the cover. Strangely the door was coming nearer, and Prince was now standing, sturdily balanced, wagging his thick tail. I flailed with my arms and legs. I didn't want to go under, because I'd already swallowed mouthfuls of water as the current swirled about me and I was frightened that I wouldn't surface again.

The raft lunged closer, and then came a surprise that made me feel, for the first time since I thought I'd cut my finger, that things would possibly improve. For behind Prince I made out a figure at the other end of the raft. I couldn't see much in the darkness, but the shape was familiar. A girl. She called out, "Hold on!" And even though she was shouting, I knew the voice— purposeful and bright despite the danger. She knelt upright, steering the raft with a long prop snatched from a washing line. "Hang on to this," she called, as the pole poked into my chest. "Grab hold. Pull yourself aboard!" I did, though it wasn't easy clambering on to the door, which was pitching about violently. My arms were heavy and my legs weak, and my saturated pyjamas dragged at my limbs. She helped haul me up, and Prince tried to lick my face. I found the brass door handle to hang on to and coughed up what seemed to be a bucketful of slime.

I haven't mentioned Sylvia. I didn't know she was coming into this story. I'm glad she did. She was the same age as me, but lived some distance from the village, so I didn't see her much except at school. She and I won everything between us. When I was allowed to see my school reports the first thing I looked for was the position and mark for each subject. I didn't read the teacher's spidery comments until later. If I was first in a subject, I knew Sylvia would have come second. If I'd got 94%—the marking was like that—I knew she'd be on around 92%. If I wasn't first, I was second: I might have 91%. I knew Sylvia would have come top with, say, 97%. (I want to give her higher marks than me because, as you will see, she deserves them.) So between us we beat all the others in everything, except Needlework, which I couldn't do.

In our first year at school she and I read every book there was. I hadn't realised this until she said she'd only one more to read. When I looked along the shelves, I discovered the same applied to me. So we had a race. Unfortunately, at the next Reading Time, the book I needed was taken by someone else. To tell you the truth it was one of those books about Janet and John and Rover, and it was so simple I hadn't bothered with it. So Sylvia won, and I was a bit annoyed about it for a day or two, but she said it was a dead heat really because she knew I read lots of books at home, where she didn't have many. That's what she was like, really nice.

Sometimes after school a few of us would wander

round the village, not planned or anything, just as the mood took us. Usually we went straight home, but there were days when, for no especial reason, we'd sit in a field or go for a walk through the woods, that sort of thing. One day we'd gone, about eight of us I should think, down a lane that led to a farm. I don't know who suggested it, or whether someone turned along it on a whim and the rest of us followed. It must have been early autumn, because there was a fresh haystack in the farmyard. The corn glowed, really golden, not like it would be after a few months, dowdy and sodden. The boys started turning cartwheels. You do that, obviously, in farmyards. I didn't though, because I wasn't much good at them. I watched a while, then looked across at the girls. Most things like that we did in separate groups. Boys were dirty and clumsy and noisy. Girls wore dresses and were pretty and kept themselves neat.

They were taking turns at handstands, seeing how straight they could make them and how long they could hold them while the others counted. I saw Sylvia's fingers braced in the dust, hands moulded to the cobbles. Her long golden hair should have been next, but she must have tied it back. Instead came the hem of her dress, and the faded blue of the inside of the skirt, flopping over her head. Then there was a strip of brown tummy, her navy knickers, and above those her long legs reaching up. They were white around the thighs, but got darker until they were this rich honey colour. She'd kicked off her shoes and socks and I could see wisps of straw sticking to her feet. Her feet weren't scratched and grubby like mine.

She was still there when I remembered I was supposed to collect the milk from the farm, so it was just as well we'd gone down that lane, because I'd forgotten. When I left the dairy, I took the short cut across the fields and didn't pass the haystack. I expect I heard the boys shouting and whooping, but didn't pay attention to them. I was daring myself to swing the churn over without its lid. Centrifugal force, another theory.

I think that was the last time I saw Sylvia. I'm pretty sure she wasn't at school again, and early the next year she died. Nobody mentioned it, not even outside school. It would have been bad luck. Another of us might have died if we'd talked about it. I had that last memory of her, so of course it became mixed up with her death. Sometimes I believed I was watching when her arms gave way and she fell on to her head, breaking her neck or cracking her skull. I imagined it lots of times. But that couldn't have been how she died, because the others would have said. They'd have run to the farm for help, and P.C. Anderson would have been alerted.

I do think of her walking the mile-and-a-half home on that beautiful evening, though. I wonder if she felt dizzy after being upside down for so long—she was better at handstands than the others. She would have felt a bit funny when she got home, gone to bed early with a headache. I never knew why she died. I don't suppose it was a mystery. The doctors and her family would have known, but, as I've said, it wasn't talked about in front of children. She didn't have any brothers or sisters, so there were no whispered secrets in the playground.

I'm glad she's paddled into this story, because I missed her. I think I was in love with her, if I could be at that age. I liked being with her, warm and eager, and I think that, as far as a girl would admit, she might have liked me, too.

It's odd, the three of us. I can understand seeing Prince's ghost, because I've imagined him so often carrying me round the yard. And I do recall what he looked like (glossy black, tubby, with great thick legs). But it's strange about Sylvia, because I was only five when I read The Flood on that terrible night, and she couldn't have died until she was eight. Perhaps she's always been living those first few years, not anticipating any others.

And I'm sorry but I know nothing else about the raft, or how I came to write this story. But I must have come to my senses, and I certainly woke my ideas up, though I don't suppose in the way my father would have wished.

Sylvia wants you to decide on these things for yourselves: did we stay on the raft much longer? How long did it take for the water to go down and the world to dry out? It always does you know: think of Noah and his homing pigeons. And she'd like some ideas on where you think she is now. She says a map showing rivers and ocean currents might help, but I think she's teasing.

She's in only one other of these stories, though in a sense she's in them all. And I've some theories of my own for you, about switching off lights, turning off taps and opening windows, and how to keep magic inside books, where it belongs.

SILENCE

September 1945

It wasn't fair. He was only four. Everyone knew you started school at five. Derek was four as well, but he didn't have to go to school: he was allowed to stay at home. It wasn't fair.

"Walk properly, Roy. Don't scuff your feet. You'll ruin those shoes." Good, thought Roy, then I'd have to go back home.

But the school gate was near, and beyond it were children running and shouting, though always leaving a space around a stern-looking lady, who was coming towards him. She held a whistle in one hand.

"Good morning, Miss Burton," his mother said. The gate opened and Roy was thrust inside. "Say 'Good Morning' to Miss Burton, Roy. Remember your manners." He knew the warning tone of voice, but couldn't speak. "Roy—"

"Don't worry, Mrs. Newsome. It's just nerves. We've a few new children this term. It takes them different ways. I'm sure Roy will settle down soon enough."

No he won't, Roy decided.

The whistle shrilled in his ears. He turned, but the gate was closed, and his mother had already disappeared behind the beech hedge that bordered it. Miss Burton led him to the front of the queue lining up outside the building.

"Silence! Before we go in, I want you to remember that there are several new children joining us today. I expect Standard Four monitors to help them with their coats and show them their pegs, then take them to my classroom ready for the register. Lead in."

Roy found himself next to a burly boy who wore heavy boots, long trousers and a pullover with a hole in the sleeve. "My name's Brian. Wha's yourn?"

Roy supposed the last remark must be Brian's surname.

Brian continued, "Alright, be like that. I dun't care," and shoved Roy through the porch into a corridor. For the next few minutes Roy battled through a maze of legs, arms and overcoats. Bodies jostled until, miraculously, every child was standing by a desk.

"For this week I'll take the register for all of you in the senior classroom," said Miss Burton. "Then you will get to know each other. When your name is called, you're to reply, 'Here, miss!' loudly and clearly."

Roy knew some of the surnames, but none of the children, who duly responded as required. But he had found the silence in the line outside the door the most appealing sensation of the morning so far—better than the drag of feet in the gravel on the way to school, than the squeaky gate, than his mother's voice that hadn't said goodbye, than the roaring children in the playground, and much, much better than the piercing whistle blown by Miss Burton. Thus, when his name was called, he said nothing. And a second time, nothing.

"I know he's here. I've already spoken to him," said Miss Burton, without looking up.

I might not be, though, Roy thought. I might still be outside, or running back down the road. Anyway, you didn't speak to me, you spoke to my mum, so I'm not going to speak to you.

After the register the younger children were shepherded into the second classroom to be taught by Miss Darby. Roy took no notice of anything going on there, and at playtime stood motionless by the playground gate. Even on the crocodile march to the church hall for dinner he didn't speak. This was, additionally, because his partner was a girl whose complexion and clothing were the colour of mushy peas, and he certainly didn't want to say anything to her. And, despite the giggles of the rest of the children, throughout the entire day he spoke to no one, not even to his mother when she came to the gate to collect him. Only when passing Derek's house, next door to his own, did he break silence. "It's not fair," he said.

His mother walked with him to school on the second day. The ash trees sighed with the promise of the day to come, full of sunshine. The leaves were tinged with orange and the grass verges offered a pathway to the fields where he and his mother had sometimes taken a picnic. As they rounded the last corner the voices from the playground welled up.

"They all seem to be enjoying themselves," his mother said. Roy sniffed. "Make sure you behave yourself and answer when you're spoken to."

As she turned from him, his resolve tightened. He didn't return Miss Burton's welcoming smile. Smiling might have unfixed his lips, and he wasn't going to risk that. He jutted out his lower lip in a sulk that deterred other children from speaking to him. By morning playtime, they had given up trying to make him react by pulling faces, and lost interest.

On Wednesday there was singing. He liked music, and had a good sense of pitch. Each child was asked to sing up and down a scale played on the piano by Miss Darby. She spoke sternly to a boy who was too shy to sing, and rapped her ruler on the top of the piano when another was out of tune. When Roy's turn came there was a stir in the class—a few murmurs and shifting of positions as everyone tried to see. For Roy, singing quite simply wasn't speaking, so he opened his mouth and delivered all the notes in one breath. "Splendid!" said Miss Darby. She gave him a higher scale, and he completed that with ease. "What a lovely voice! And all of it in tune," she warbled. "Ten out of ten." Thirty-two out of thirty-two, Roy thought, but still didn't say anything.

Miss Darby was absent on Friday, so both classes were taught together in Miss Burton's room. The older boys carried in extra chairs and placed them to make three at each double desk. Roy had to sit next to Brian. He squeezed himself in at the end of the desk and spent much of the morning avoiding Brian's fidgety elbow. There was no relief from it at playtime, as it was raining and everyone was kept indoors.

The dinnertime crocodile splashed through the rain so that the afternoon was redolent with the smell of damp clothing. As time wore on the children became more and more restless. At one point a scuffle broke out between two older boys, whom Miss Burton struggled to part. By the time the sun broke through in the afternoon, the teacher was in as bad a mood as many of her pupils. "Be quiet!" she shouted. "If you don't quieten down I shall keep you all indoors, even though the sun's coming out." This threat resulted in improved behaviour.

"That's better. Now, the last lesson of the week is always story-time," said Miss Burton. "This story is about the war. There are sad things in the story but it does have a happy ending. Brian, please stop scraping your chair." Brian snorted noisily. "And do use a handkerchief!"

"Ain't got one, Miss." He wiped his nose on his sleeve with an exaggerated sweep of his arm, which pushed Roy off his chair, giving rise to a ripple of laughter.

"Sit still, Roy. And behave, Brian. As one of the older ones you should be setting an example. Now I will read the story, without further interruption."

Brian sprawled in his chair, his posture suggesting total indifference.

As the story progressed, chairs were shunted back, arms splayed across desk-tops and heads dropped. Roy liked the beginning of the story, where a family hid from the advancing German army, but soon Miss Burton's voice droned like the aeroplane the young boy in the story could hear as it passed overhead, and in the stuffy air of the classroom he lost track of how the family became separated. He jolted to attention when Miss Burton closed the book with a snap. "Now children," she said as the class stretched and shuffled into wakefulness. "It has been a difficult day, so to make up for having to spend so much time indoors I am going to allow you to play outside until it's time to go home."

Several children started from their desks.

"Wait! Sit down. First, those of you who listened to the story will be able to answer a few questions."

There was a collective groan.

From the questions Roy gathered that somehow the family had been reunited after various adventures. A girl sitting several places in front of him was the only one prepared to answer. Each time she raised her hand her long, golden hair swung from side to side.

"Very good, Sylvia. I'm glad somebody was listening throughout. Now, someone else, please. Who can name five of our Allies?"

There was silence.

"Come along. Wake up. Which countries fought with us in the war?"

Nobody spoke. Roy could not believe it. Miss Burton voiced his thoughts. "Surely you must know at least some of the nations who came to our aid?"

Brian stirred, thrusting his arm in the air. "Please miss?"

"Yes, Brian. Good. Go on."

"Miss, it were Italy, Japan and—" Some older members of the class burst out laughing.

"Be quiet! How dare you! You should be ashamed of yourselves. Right, the whole class will stay in for the rest of the afternoon. I've never known such disrespect. Brian, you are a wicked boy. Silence! If there is not total silence, I shall keep you in after four o'clock."

Roy tentatively raised his hand.

"Yes, Roy?—"

At the mention of his name, several faces turned towards him, some regarding him with surprise.

"Canada," he said.

There were murmurs as more children twisted in their chairs to look at him.

"Miss! Say 'Miss' when you speak to a teacher."

"Miss."

"That's better. Canada is correct. That's one. Can you tell the class any of the others? Speak up."

"Australia, Miss."

"Good. Continue."

"New Zealand and South Africa."

"Miss!"

"Miss."

"That's four. One more, somebody else?" There was no response. "Nobody?" There was a short silence. "Very well."

Then Sylvia put up her hand.

"Can you name a fifth, Sylvia?"

"Um, India, Miss."

"Very good, Sylvia. At least there are two among you who know to whom we are indebted, to whom we owe our lives. And what do those countries have in common?"

Roy was about to answer when Sylvia again raised her hand.

"The Commonwealth, Miss."

"Excellent. Yes, they are all members of the British Commonwealth. Perhaps, Brian, you can show everybody where they are on the map?"

Brian sighed and lumbered to his feet. He leant against the wall by the large map of the world, regarded it for a moment, and stuck his finger into the middle of Europe.

"No, Brian. You have not paid attention. Stand up straight."

"Says Australia, Miss."

Miss Burton moved across to him. "Brian, you have pointed out Austria."

"Says Australia," he repeated.

"Don't contradict me. Look carefully and you'll see the difference in the spelling. And in any case, you should know that Commonwealth countries are coloured in red."

"Colour blind, Miss. Always 'ave bin." There were hoots of laughter.

Miss Burton rounded on the class. "Any more of that and I shall bring out the cane. I shall be speaking to your mother, Brian, about your behaviour and your attitude. Both will have to improve considerably before you start at the new secondary school in Shefford."

"Shan't be goin.'"

"Miss!"

"Shan't be goin'," he repeated.

"Of course you'll be going. Back to your place."

Brian stood straight. "Me Dad says it won't be built in time fer the likes o' me."

"It's the law now, Brian. All of you who are over eleven will be going next year. There will be no more of this nonsense. Back to your place! I am ashamed that it took two of our youngest children to show any interest in or knowledge of recent events. Some of you seem to think that the war took place so that you could have a day off school to go into the fields and lift potatoes."

Squeezing along the aisle Brian bumped against one or two younger ones. As he slumped into his seat he stamped on Roy's foot.

"Ow!" Roy couldn't help exclaiming.

"I take it that was your doing, Brian. You will stay indoors for the rest of the afternoon."

She turned back to her desk.

Brian muttered out of the side of his mouth. "Made yer say summat, din't I?"

"Thanks to Sylvia and Roy," Miss Burton continued,

"you can all play outside for the remainder of the afternoon. Brian, collect the extra chairs and take them back to Miss Darby's room. The rest of you file out quietly into the playground, one row at a time. When I blow the whistle, it will be home time. Remember to collect your coats from the cloakroom."

The children shuffled out. Miss Burton smiled as Roy passed her in the doorway, but she didn't speak.

Brian, carrying two chairs, followed him out of the room and stumbled into him. "Git out the way, little show-off." He kicked Roy on the shin. "'N don't try gettin' me in ter trouble no more." He blundered through the file of children and barged into the other classroom.

Ahead of Roy, Sylvia's hair shone in the sunlight as she walked into the playground. He rubbed his shin where he knew a bruise would form. He decided to walk it off rather than stand in his usual place by the gate. He passed a line of girls, already performing handstands against the wall. Sylvia was waiting her turn, tying up her hair. He caught her eye, and she smiled. There was somebody, he thought, who he could talk to. And he would.

OLYMPIANS

May 1949

His shadow bounced before him across the ditch and up the bank. He was poised a stride behind the leader as they entered the final stretch. Six miles of gruelling plough and woodland were behind him, and for the last mile he had moved steadily through the field, passing the big names, avoiding trailing legs and swinging arms until he was close behind the ginger head and freckled legs of his next-door neighbour.

The tape in sight, Roy clenched his fists, rose on his toes and sprinted. The acceleration brought him alongside Davies, who countered by lengthening his stride. Don't look down, don't look right! Ahead, the worn path atop the verge curved like a railway line. Water spouted under the bridge where the path ended. Roy leant into the bend, cutting through the sharp sunlight. As long as he didn't look at Davies he could defeat him. Each pace shuddered through his calves; there was pain in the arms and shoulders as his breathing tightened. He could give in now, slither to the ground in dramatic defeat, fifteen yards short of the line, and let the whole field pass him until the Red

Cross wrapped him in blankets and carried him from the stadium. But if he succumbed, he knew he would never race again.

He heard Davies' chest wheezing, the voiced exhalations. His rival was fighting back! Deep down, he found a final surge of energy. Eight more strides... He flung himself at the bridge, collapsing face-down on the lush grass. His torso heaved, each breath the roar of a jubilant crowd. He raised a hand above his head in acknowledgement.

Newsome has won! Davies, reigning World Champion, finishes a split second behind, beaten by this phenomenal athlete. What a marvellous performance from Newsome! It's Zatopek and Pirie third and fourth, about twenty seconds behind. We'll confirm the exact times later. Davies, a brave, exhausted loser, staggers across to congratulate Newsome. He's shaking hands with his victor, now sprawled on the inside of the track...

The crowd cheers on as Roy's panting subsides. The shadow of an interviewer falls across him. "Thought yer mum weren't lettin' you out. Took yer long enuff ter get 'ere din't it?"

"I had to fill the copper this morning. I always do some jobs first. Don't you?"

"Ner! Jist be a nuisance. Drop a plate or summat'n they kick me out soon enuff."

Roy rolled over, his chest and stomach damp. He squinted up. Derek's face was a dark smudge, with a fiery halo of ginger hair. "You're just saying that, about breaking things."

"Betcha"

"Bet you don't."

"Betcha I do then, see!"

Roy lifted himself onto his elbows. His thighs bore patterns of the grass. He sat up and rubbed at them. Little rolls of sweat hardened in his palms.

"Saw yer runnin'."

"Where from?" Had the crowd noises carried?

"I was in the 'edge, in the ol' den, waitin'."

Nobody remembered who first fashioned the den. House, hospital, castle, prison, stockade and bunker, it had been a favourite meeting-place, but too many adults passed it nowadays for it to attract the older children. They had more adventurous lairs, known only to themselves and an occasional farm worker or poacher. Some hides were up trees, accessible only to the better climbers, others in haystacks, orchards, bramble-patches; the more difficult the location, the more prestigious. Roy scorned the crows'-nests, burrowing hollows in thick hedges or tunnelling through the tangled undergrowth of the further woods.

"Seen anyone else?" He twisted to look down the road and then along the cinder path that bordered the cartway beside the hedge.

"Nar. Mick 'ad ter go shoppin'. En't seen none o' the others."

This was unexpected: the day after Whit Monday, the rest of the week a holiday, and the late spring sky deepening around a strengthening sun.

"Perhaps they're hiding."

"P'raps."

"Come on then."

They scuffed along the path, kicking congealed clumps of cinders, swishing overhanging branches on one side and pausing to indent sponges of soft mud on the other. When, a couple of hundred yards further, a favourite tree concealed neither pirates nor Indian scouts, the search was tacitly abandoned. Derek had already lagged behind. Turning, Roy saw him standing on one leg, trailing his other foot through the sludgy remains of a puddle. He walked back. Derek had ploughed a large D in the mud. His shoe was caked in squelchy clay.

"There are some tadpoles in Barclay's Pond," Roy suggested. "They're growing legs."

"Wait a minute."

"What?"

Derek pivoted from the puddle and flicked his foot at Roy, splattering him with dark brown flecks.

"Hey, stop it!"

"Goal!" Derek kicked more mud.

"Quit it!" Dirt was strictly rationed, if not by himself then by an irate mother who at that very moment was scrubbing and wringing her way through the weekly wash.

"Another 'n!" Derek screamed. "'E's on 'is way to an 'at-trick."

"He isn't! He'll get injured and be carted off on a stretcher."

"Betcha!"

Roy turned and walked off. Derek followed, lurching

to preserve as much mud as possible on his shoe. Roy trotted, but Derek speeded up, hopping wildly. "'E's on a run down the left wing; 'e's dribbled past the full-back. 'E's got a ninjury, but it won't stop 'im."

Roy heard his lumbering step behind.

"'E's roundin' the goalie: 'e's left 'im on 'is arse in the mud. 'E's shootin'—it's another goal!" He stopped the impetus of the swing to project the mud. His other foot slipped on a tussock. He fell over just as a lump of sodden earth flew from his instep to hit Roy fully in the small of the back.

"Stop it, I said!"

"Ow! It 'urts," Derek groaned, clutching his ankle.

"Serves you right." Roy could see the washing line flapping its semaphore at him from his back garden across the field. Furiously, he pulled the shirt over his head. "Look what you've done!"

"Wha'bout my ankle?"

"Your own fault. Serves you bloody well right!" Roy's rare expletive emphasised the gravity of the situation. The two glared at each other. A slight breeze ruffled the branches; Roy shivered.

"It 'urts."

"Hard luck." Roy out-stared him.

Derek grimaced, shifted his position, vigorously rubbing his ankle.

Roy held the shirt out before him: exhibit A. "Mum'll go mad when she sees this."

"Cissy."

"I'm not!"

"Yis y'are. Mummy's boy."

"Just 'cos I don't go around smashing things and kicking mud over everyone."

"Yer a cissy."

"Well you wait 'til she finds out it was you."

"Tell-tale tit. Say yer fell over. If yer tell on me, we'll get yer."

"You and whose army?"

"All on us. When they know yer been splittin' on us."

"Us! Well, just you wait. She'll go round your house as soon as I get home."

Derek stood up to deliver his trump card. "'N Brian'll get yer 'n all. 'E's goin' out wiv me sister 'n 'e's always round our 'ouse, so there." Brian was now eighteen and drove a tractor, on which he daily delivered milk for Mr. Jenkinson. It was a moment in the early morning when Roy made sure he was nowhere near the back door. Derek limped onto the path. He wiped at a smear of blood, cleaning his hand on his trousers.

"You're a cripple. You couldn't get anyone." Then, before that theory could be tested, Roy added quickly, "Anyway I don't know why we came here. The rest of them aren't around, are they?"

"'Oo said they was?" rejoined Derek. "I were comin' up 'ere anyway."

"What for?"

"Secret."

"Don't care."

"I'll show yer."

"Still don't care."

"In that tree there." He pointed to an oak a short distance away. It had no low branches.

"What's up there then?" Roy asked, casually. He was poor at shinning, usually failing to gain sufficient height and grazing his knees in the attempt.

"Guess."

"Branches and leaves."

"Clever-dick. What else?"

"Bird-shit."

Derek giggled. "'Spect there is. Last guess."

Roy peered into the black and emerald tapestry. He could discern nothing out of the ordinary. He noticed a few high clouds, white and fluffy like the cotton wool used for dabbing knees. He imagined the smell of antisceptic taken from the cupboard under the stairs. "A new den."

"Tha's right! 'Sa secret—jist fer me.

Roy stared up, his shirt hanging over one arm. "What do you want one there for?"

"Spy on the littl'uns from up there, can't I? You can an' all, if yer want."

With that, ankle forgotten, Derek dashed to the tree and leapt at the trunk, clinging to it like some insect. "C'm on," he called. "'Seasy." He wriggled upwards, fingers stretching to the first branch. Leaning out, he scaled with his feet, his hands moving along the branch until his body was horizontal. He swung his leg over the branch and levered his body to lie along it. He grinned down at Roy. "Me Tarzan," he said. "Come up 'ere 'n' I'll show yer."

Roy was silent. The face beamed down at him, darkly freckled against the foliage.

"If yer get this 'igh yer can jist see it."

Roy hesitated.

"'S not 'ard," continued Derek, with a note of condescension.

"If you can see it from there it's not worth it. It won't stay secret for long."

"Yeah, but the litl'uns wun't get up 'ere, will they?"

Roy felt his face reddening. "I can't," he said at last. "I'm holding this." He displayed the muddy shirt, like a flag.

"Cissy." Derek jeered. "I said yer were a cissy'n so y'are."

The sunlight weakened momentarily behind the fringes of a cloud.

"I could get up there if I wanted to."

"Go orn… Yer a cissy."

"I don't want to get all scratched, and my shirt's wet through with that mud."

"Wha' a nat-trick!" Derek gloated.

"Anyway, I can see it from here."

"Wha'?"

"Your den. I can see it, right up there."

"Liar."

"There."

"Where?"

"A bit to the left, up above you." Roy picked out a spot far overhead, where two thick limbs overlapped.

"Well yer wrong, clever-stick, 'n yer a cissy, 'cos there ain't no den 'n yer jist sayin' that, see?" Derek allowed his body to swing from the branch, feet and hands locked around it. "Cissy, cissy!" he sang, swaying from side to side in time. "Mummy's little pet. Cissy, cissy! Mummy's little pet."

"Well it looks like a sort of den from here, and if there isn't one then why're you swinging about like a gorilla?"

"…Mummy's little pet." Cackling, Derek came to a rest for a moment. Then he hauled himself once again on top of the branch. "Me Tarzan," he concluded, looking down. "You Jane."

Roy's head sank: he looked at his shirt, then dropped his arms to his sides. Partially covered by long grass at the fringe of the track he saw a smooth, oval stone, the size of an egg, probably churned there by a tractor.

"Well there is a secret, see!" taunted Derek. "But I've a good mind ter keep it ter meself seein's yer sich a coward."

"Keep it, for all I care."

Derek resumed his chant, less raucous, but more measured. He added another phrase. "Cowardy-cowardy custard. Cissy, cissy, cowardy-cowardy custard." It became fainter, muffled, and broken up with grunts and bursts of rustling.

When Roy looked up again, Derek was out of sight. "What are you doing?" he called, despite himself. He scratched at the cinders on the path, becoming absorbed in the earth, noticing again the oval stone.

Derek had returned to his perch. "Look at this, then. Me find treasure." Precariously he reached down, one arm outstretched. In his hand was an egg, sky-blue with dark speckles. "'S what I really came fer, see? Den my foot!" He giggled. "'S if anyone'd bother ter make a den up 'ere. There's three more of 'em. Found 'em on Friday, arter school. No one else knows, 'part from you, 'n you en't even seen 'em yit." His ginger head, inverted, was as freckled as the egg. "Reach up, so's I can give it yer."

"I don't collect them."

"Well I does. 'Old it fer me while I git the rest. I can't climb down wiv 'em."

Roy froze. He could no sooner help someone go bird-nesting than do it himself. He just couldn't. Derek's eyes were riveted upon him. Slowly he stretched towards Derek, keeping his elbow a little crooked. "I'm not tall enough."

"Stretch yer arm proper."

"I am."

"No yer not. Go orn, reach." The face glared down at him as the sun went in completely. Ugly things, things from nightmares, things that lurk in the pitch black of night were leering, snarling down. Roy slowly straightened his arm, at the same time bending his knees a little.

Derek slackened the grip of his legs so that his arm hung lower. There was still a gap of some eighteen inches. "Catch it then."

Before Roy could readjust the egg was tumbling through the air. He was a good catcher, and although he was hindered by the shirt over his arm he grabbed, one-handed. Anxious to somehow preserve the life inside, he clenched his fingers as the egg touched his palm. Yolk squirted into his face. He could feel the stickiness on his forehead. One eye closed as the fluid ran down. He bent over to clear his vision, and to wipe the mess from his hand on the grass. The red-head was shrieking. "There's yer custard, cowardy."

Roy saw that yolk had spilt onto his shirt, merging with the mud. He flung the garment onto the cinders in exasperation. Still stooping, unable to look at Derek, he raged. "You filthy blighter! Now look what you've done. You thieving, stinking, filthy—" There was no point continuing against the deluge of yells and whoops from above. He reached for his shirt. Next to it, on the fringe of the path, was the oval stone. He snatched it, straightened, looked up at Derek attempting to regain a sitting posture on the branch, brought his arm from behind his back and hurled the stone. It flew straight and hard, like a startled partridge. The cackling stopped abruptly. There was a shout, then silence, stillness.

Roy grabbed his shirt and ran. There was a thud behind him. Don't stop. Don't look back. The cinders spurted from the thrust of his feet. The sun was still behind cloud. The air felt cold on his bare torso.

And after his unexpected success in the hammer, Newsome leads the field in the mile. Davies is several yards back, looking beaten. Zatopek and Peters are gaining ground on him, the three of them bunched on the final curve. But it's Newsome entering the straight, forging ahead. Newsome's winning by ten, twelve yards. He's surely going to smash the Olympic record. What an athlete this man is! The real race is for second place—good heavens! Davies is down! Was he spiked? He's lying on the track: he's not getting up. But let's enjoy this wonderful run by Newsome. He's approaching the tape, he breaks it... now! He's won by a huge margin, with Zatopek I think just edging out Peters for second place. Davies is still motionless, but he was back in fourth before he fell, yet again thwarted by his clubmate who this season has become absolutely invincible...

MERVYN

September 1950

"Where're you going? There's no path on that side," Roy called.

"'Oo needs a path!"

Roy followed him, not letting it rest. "Why've you crossed here?"

"Always do."

"What for?"

Mervyn paused, picked up a discarded stick, then turned to look at Roy. He twiddled the length of elder between his palms. "Ter keep away from that ol' witch." He nodded towards the cottage opposite. Mrs. Plover's thatched roof warmed in the sun behind a hedge of brambles. The ruby blackberries hung heavy with cobwebs; beyond them her gnarled trees stood motionless in the heaviness of mid-September.

"She's alright," protested Roy. Mrs. Plover was one of the village's elderly spinsters who tolerated well-behaved small boys. Roy had even been invited to sample her dandelion wine, which he thought tasted horrible, and to stroke several cats who were draped over the cushions piled around her. He remembered the dim front room, cool but cosy with its velvet and old pine.

"I tell yer, she's a witch," Mervyn muttered darkly.

Mervyn held his own opinions on things that concerned him, offering no viewpoint on those that didn't. To encounter him was unusual; to walk with him through the village, rare. If not alone, he preferred to spend time with his older cousin, Brian, whom Roy had taken pains to avoid since his first week at school. He sometimes glimpsed the pair of them tramping the hedgerows or stealing into the woods, heads lowered, backs bent and a couple of sacks tied round their waists. To accompany Mervyn was dangerous. His unorthodox pastimes and mischievous nature made the pattern of the day unpredictable, so Roy, despite being several months older, never felt in control of events when in his presence.

They recrossed the road past the orchard gate, where a raised strip of asphalt denoted the path. Roy heard the gate scrape open behind him. He turned to see Mrs. Plover's white hair showing through the brambles, and one of her eyes glaring out. His smile froze as the rest of her face came into view. "An' yer can keep that stick o' yourn orf o' me apples!" she shouted, as if concluding a conversation.

Too late for 'Hello-Mrs-Plover-how-are-you?' Anyway, her stare was fixed on Mervyn.

"No one wants yer rotten apples, Cat-lady!" Mervyn stared defiantly back.

"You wun't 'ave 'em, that's fer sure, yer cheeky divil."

"You're the only one 'oo's sour enuff fer 'em," Mervyn taunted, approaching her.

Roy was horrified: he knew that if he behaved in that manner he would soon be in trouble. He wouldn't insult any adult, especially one who had shown him kindness. The most serious challenge to authority he had mounted had been to remain silent throughout his first week at school. That was several years ago, though he was still occasionally reminded of it. But now circumstances made him an accessory. If, as seemed likely, this incident was to develop, the whole village might hear of it—and thus, eventually, his father. However peripheral his part in the drama, he would better avoid what threatened to be a painful outcome. At the same time, his age demanded loyalty to Mervyn. And Roy was wary of his grasp of a wider world, his older cousin. Mervyn could make a frightening enemy.

Mrs. Plover also appeared indecisive, while Mervyn continued his assault. "Yer sich 'n 'ol crab yerself," he jeered, "yer ought ter git up them there trees wiv' 'em."

The old lady gasped. She shook the upright stakes of the gate, rattling the latch. "You wicked boy! Whatever your mother was, she did right ter leave yer." With that, she turned, slammed the gate to and vanished behind her hedge.

The silence that followed was full of questions. Roy hadn't dared look at Mervyn earlier, lest he laugh. He didn't feel like laughing now. Mervyn's face was white.

Normally, his olive skin was swarthy. It was another feature that set him apart.

Mervyn wheeled away without speaking. Roy followed until they reached the playing-field. It was customary that, on entering the field and sighting the pair of swings in the corner beyond the cricket boundary, the children raced each other to them. Roy was glad of the opportunity to change the atmosphere. He sped across the field, leapt on a swing and was already soaring higher than the hawthorn hedge before he realised he had not been pursued.

Mervyn was instead hobbling down the edge of the field, leaning on his stick which, when he saw Roy was watching, he raised threateningly. He twisted his face into a grotesque imitation of the old lady. Roy could almost see the gate wobbling as Mervyn thrust his free hand back and forth. "You bin at my blackberries 'n all. I'll 'ave yer in a pie!" he shrieked.

Roy thrust with his legs to make the swing sail higher than its frame. Mervyn stood before the other swing, bending over earth worn bare by the feet of generations of children. He used his stick to draw in the dust, his lips moving with concentration. With the squeak of the chains Roy could not tell if Mervyn was muttering, but there was certainly a precision in the figures and shapes he glimpsed on each pass over Mervyn's shoulder. Roy slowed until he could brake with his feet, and, as he did so, Mervyn obliterated the design with the toe of his boot. The last segment of a circle vanished as Mervyn stood upright.

"D'yer want ter come wiv me?"

"Where to?"

"I'm goin' back."

"What, home?" Roy had never entered Mervyn's house. If he did, would he learn more of his past? A photo of the missing mother? Or some clue as to 'whatever' instead of 'whoever' she had been?

"I'm goin' back ter the witch's," Mervyn explained. "I might go 'ome after. Yer can come with me ter 'er orchard if yer want, but yer dun't 'ave to." He smoothed over the patch of dust, then firmed it with his heel.

Roy considered the alternatives. He could stay with his companion, which would mean some involvement in the next episode—it was evident that there would be a sequel—or he could go home, thereby disclaiming any connection with whatever elapsed. His instinct told him to let Mervyn go, for he knew he himself could hardly be in any bother yet. Mrs. Plover probably hadn't even noticed him, so intent was she on her antagonist. But Mervyn had charisma, and even the small insights into his world that Roy had glimpsed today were fascinating.

Mervyn was indeed different. Even among the older children, his escapades were legendary—his daring, his scrapes, his cheek. Roy could witness the making of a new fable. And if there was trouble at the end of it all, perhaps it would be worth it for the excitement alone; and then, later, there would be the glory of it as he told and re-told the epic to the others… Mind you, Mervyn had made it clear that Roy wasn't needed. What would he think of him if he abandoned the whole thing? He played for time.

"What did she mean?"

"Wha' about?"

"When she said, you know... What she said about your mother?" Why couldn't he have said 'mum'?

"I told yer, she's bad. She jist says things."

"Yeah, but you live with your cousin, don't you?"

"So what?"

"Well, I don't live with a cousin."

"'Ave yer got a cousin?"

"No."

"Well, there y'are then." With that he pivoted forwards off his stick and strode towards the far corner of the field, swishing at dandelion heads as he went. Roy had to decide: the story was about to unfold without him.

"Martin!" It came out louder than intended. Mervyn stopped dead. For seconds nothing moved in the field, except for the sway of the abandoned swing. Even from a distance there was something about the young figure stooping over the gnarled stick that brought an ache to Roy's throat. It struck him for the first time that despite the entry in the school register—which Roy, as monitor, daily laid open on her desk—not even Miss Burton used that name.

Mervyn turned slowly to face Roy. He lifted his free hand and beckoned. Roy trod the distance between them with trepidation. He even counted the paces—

fifty-two. Each step, he felt, marked the differences between them. How many miles would it take to account for them all?

"My name is Mervyn."

Roy stared at the face before him: creased, walnutty, seemingly centuries old. The eyes had watered, the expression was fierce.

"My name is always Mervyn."

Roy nodded. Mervyn held Roy's gaze. Roy felt the black pupils scorching into him. He bit his lip. Again, Mervyn turned. The decision had somehow been taken.

On the way to the orchard, Roy pondered on how adults reacted to his companion. He had never seen the Cat-lady angry, or heard her speak as she had just now. Yet Miss Burton, who must have investigated that entry in the register, was always lenient with Mervyn, meting out far lighter punishment for his misdemeanours than was endured by others for lesser offences. Had he been clever at schoolwork this might be better understood, but he was at least as lazy as the slowest pupil, often distracting others with his pranks. Much of his time was spent day-dreaming or doodling, muttering almost inaudibly to himself or even, on occasion, quite simply falling asleep. Yet he was never given more than a few lines to write out. Whereas Roy, normally alert and interested, would find himself digging the heavy clay of the vegetable plot in the blistering sunshine, washing the windows that could safely be reached, or, in winter months, shovelling scuttles of coke into the boiler, all punishments to be remembered long after the petty infringements that incurred them. (Oddly, it now occurred to him, such tasks were also referred to by Miss Burton as privileges for the older ones when no offenders offered themselves).

They stopped level with the corner of the orchard.

"Stay there, out o' sight."

Roy stepped onto the verge and made a space in the brambles. Mervyn swaggered on until he reached the gate. To Roy, his next action was astounding. He kicked at the gate, kicked again when it refused to fully open, and strolled through. The loosened catch fell. In no time he was among trees, haphazardly striking lower branches. Several crab-apples fell, with tufts of leaves and twigs. Mervyn picked one up, stood with legs astride in full view of the tiny window in the gable end and tossed it casually into the thatch of the roof. A sparrow flew out. He guffawed. His movements were larger than life. He rampaged around, thrashing at random. A ginger cat scuttled through the hedge only a few feet from Roy, veering when it saw him, running low with ears back and tail strung out.

The window below the eaves was pushed open. Mrs. Plover glared down. Mervyn had his back to the house, yet immediately stopped cavorting. He let out a loud roar and turned to face her. Surprisingly, it was he who spoke first. "Cat-lady, I've a-come fer yer apples." His voice was high and challenging.

"I'm a-warnin' yer, yer young scoundrel, ter keep away. Or yer'll rue it."

"I'll jist take a coupla pounds fer now. They'll make a nice tea fer me ferret."

"I'll not 'ave yer in my garden, an' if I set eyes on that weasel o' yourn I s'll wring its neck fer it. You let it roun' my garden agin an' I'll be tellin' Mr. Anderson on yer."

Roy crouched lower: mention of the village bobby conjured visions of parental retribution.

"Me ferret likes yer cats, Cat-lady, an' it likes yer apples an' all. I reckon two pounds'd be enuff ter keep it off o' yer cats."

"I s'll go straight up the road ter that policeman if yer dun't git out now."

"Go an' fetch yer broomstick, Polly-Plover. I'm pickin' these 'ere apples fer yer." He collected two from between his feet. "Try one." He bit a portion out, spat it on the grass and threw the remainder at the window. She slammed it shut and soon emerged from her cottage door, carrying a yard brush. Mervyn, unconcerned, was gathering more apples and lobbing some into the thatch. "Feed the sparrers, feed the crows," he sang.

The Cat-lady walked a few paces towards him. "Put them apples down and go."

"Feed the sparrers, feed the crows."

""Yer'll not so much as take one apple from me orchard, you gypsy you." She came nearer.

"Then I s'll take two," he countered, putting them into his pocket. "One, two."

"You varmint! You villain! Y'aint worth one o' them: there be more good in one o' them than in the 'ole o' yer evil body."

Mervyn circled her. His voice was still jubilant, and his eyes blazed.

"I'm a-goin' ter take two apples afore I goes ter bed, 'N the others I've knocked down I'll throw at Dolly-Pullover's 'ead."

Roy stifled giggles. The scene before him was in earnest. Mervyn's warrior dance encircled the Cat-lady's scything with the brush as she kept him at bay. It was like a primitive ritual, yet Mervyn's antics had Roy shivering with suppressed mirth.

"You'll take nothing from me, you brat. You shall indeed not. Y'aint fit ter live in 'n 'ouse, nor no village, even. Y'ought ter be in a caravan, or a travellin' fair, you gypsy divil. I curse you. I shall git Jacob ter take you wiv 'im."

Mervyn stopped his lunging dance. "'E en't even 'ere yit, so shows 'ow much you know."

Jacob was a tramp. Each year he arrived, rags flapping about him like a migratory bird. He took odd jobs and joined with villagers in piecework. He arrived in the village for harvest, and would be seen greasing the belts on the threshing machine, sweeping chaff into piles, raking straw and stuffing it into sacks. Jacob came with the harvest moon and, like the moon, would slip away when harvest was done, and not even the smell of his blackened old pipe would remain. He slept wherever there was shelter, in barns, back porches and haystacks, and took food in return for his labour. He was never refused or turned away, and there was no telling of a story about Jacob for there was no known beginning and no known end.

Mervyn lobbed several apples into the air. Mrs. Plover raised her brush to fend off any that might fall on her. "Cat-lady, you be like a scarecrow. You git on that brush and fly away, you ol' witch."

"How dares yer, yer snotty brat! I curse you most powerfully." She stepped towards him again, the shadows of the branches dappling her face, giving her the camouflage of some savage. They began to prowl around each other, like cats.

"Put your curse upon my 'ead,
Your kits and cats they shall be dead."

"Curse you I shall and curse you I do. Now be off." She brandished the brush.

Mervyn laughed, turned his back on her and sauntered out through the gateway. "Yer can shut it yerself, Cat-lady. Or yer can leave it open. Anyways, I s'll be back." And with that he wandered nonchalantly up the road.

Roy remained in his crouched position, peering through the brambles to watch Mrs. Plover. She closed the gate, clanging the rusty bolt against the post. She didn't appear to notice the missing latch. She paced the edge of the orchard. As she neared Roy he saw that her eyes were closed, yet she avoided low branches and bushes. She seemed oblivious to his proximity but glided down the path between her vegetable beds, reaching the cottage door. She dragged the brush across the doorstep, once to the right and once to the left, then went inside, closing the door behind her.

"See that? I told yer she were bad." Roy, still transfixed by the encounter, jumped in surprise as Mervyn squatted beside him, the thorny stems arching above him as he took the two apples from his pocket, and, leaning towards him, offered one to Roy. The sunlight slanted across Mervyn, accentuating the creases that gouged his features. For a moment Roy saw Jacob bending forward, puffing over his briar.

"Want one?"

"No—no thanks."

"Dun't blame yer: they're 'orrible."

"If I'm lucky I'll be given some good ones tonight. I'm helping decorate the church for Harvest Festival tomorrow."

"I 'opes them'll be better than these. They're sour as shit."

"Crab apples always are—I've never tasted a sweet one, anyway. What did you want them for in the first place?"

"I din't. Only to aggravate 'er. She makes jellies an' jam wiv 'em, I s'pect. I took two, jist ter spite the ol' baggage. Two seems about the right number."

After church Roy walked back alone. Often Daphne, a year younger, walked with him, but she wasn't there today. And Derek hadn't been for several weeks. They were the only other village children left in the choir. Roy was surprised the others had missed Harvest

Festival, because it was a lively service with jollier hymns than usual. He didn't mind Derek not being there, because he sang too loudly and was often out of tune, but he missed Daphne, whose frequent absences had something to do with her father.

Roy was imagining an organ extravaganza on the tune of We Plough the Fields and Scatter when he noticed a large bicycle thrown against the fence round Cottage Spinney. There was a scrambling of feet on the pales, then Mervyn's face rose above them. "Watcher, Roy."

"Hello." It seemed Mervyn had been waiting. Roy was both flattered and alarmed. Somehow there was an unbridgeable distance between the events of the previous day and having so recently been attired in cassock and surplice. And yet throughout Parson Fox's unintelligible sermon Roy's attention had been drawn time and again to a mound of fruit, centre-piece of the altar decorations. On either side of the huge silver dish piled with produce from the fields and gardens had been placed a small green apple, each positioned directly before the ceremonial candlesticks. The apples had seemed incongruous among the resplendent harvest yield. As he stared at them, vaguely wondering at their prominence, the effects of fluctuating sunlight through the stained glass, the weak electric glow and the flickering candlelight distorted his vision. The dull apples swelled and shrank, danced, hovered and bounced until he saw four of them instead of two. Then, shaking his head and looking elsewhere—at the dozing organist, the flying angels, the strands of hair down the back of the vicar's head—to clear his vision, he was drawn to them again, staring until they once more became blurred shadows. Only with the grinding bellow of the introduction to the next hymn did he blink into proper focus, when the hearts and minds and voices demanded his full concentration.

"Dun't yer get a bit bored with church an' all that?"

"Sometimes. Today was alright though, 'cause it was Harvest, so it was better than usual."

"I dun't go near the church meself. An' the vicar, 'e never comes to our 'ouse, so that's that. Suits me. I like 'arvest though. 'Specially follerin' the binder an' chasin' out the rats an' rabbits. Last year up Jensey's top field I smashed a big ol' 'are wi' me stick 'n killed it. One 'it, stone dead."

Roy's view of harvest contrasted essentially with Mervyn's. Not that that should surprise him. And Mervyn was rarely so communicative.

"You did go near the church though, didn't you? Last night?"

There was a pause before Mervyn replied. "You git some queer ideas." He picked up the bicycle and wheeled it alongside Roy. "It's me cousin's. Bit big fer me, but I can ride it. Got four gears an' all." They walked in a silence broken only by the ticking wheels. When they came to the downhill slope after Cottage Spinney Mervyn slung a leg over the saddle and freewheeled, dragging his boot in the gravel to slow to Roy's pace.

A car came up behind them. Roy turned to see Mr.

Jenkinson's Morris Eight, full of church-goers with gloves and hats. He stepped onto the grass bank to make way, but Mervyn allowed the bike to wobble from one side to the other. The old car slowed, grating through a gear-change. Mervyn's feet were kicking out at the air, his body leaning back as if on the point of toppling off. Then he swerved to one side and hovered there for a few seconds, tempting the driver to pass. Roy stayed on the bank, for the second time that weekend observing Mervyn's risky antics. The car stuttered forward—only for Mervyn to swoop across the front of it in an apparently desperate attempt to regain control. "'Elp! 'Elp!" he yelled, leaning to one side, grounding his foot then rolling into a spectacular tumble. The car stopped abruptly, its engine stalled.

"You've run him over, Albert!"

The driver's door opened. "I niver touched 'im, woman!" He leant over the mudguard and bonnet to look. The wheels of the bicycle clicked on. "You wants to learn to ride that thing proper afore you takes it on the road. You be a danger to everyone, yer young fool."

"Albert! You've knocked 'im down. Lawks-a-mussy."

Mervyn stood up and, with a dramatic stumble, limped towards the bicycle.

Mr. Jenkinson inserted the starting handle, then returned to switch the engine on. "Dun't anyone touch that gear lever or it'll knock me down."

Mervyn leant against the bicycle, rubbing his shin and running through a repertoire of anguished facial expressions.

"You should be more careful, Albert, you could've broke 'is leg."

"Drat it, woman, I told yer I never touched'm. 'E were clownin' about." His attempts to restart the car were failing, but not for want of exertion. He straightened, and, seeing Roy, passed him his jacket. "'Ere, young man, 'old on to this. And dun't go droppin' it, mind." He bent again, his upper body lunging into the heave of the handle. "Damn and blast!"

"Albert, yer've just been givin' thanks to the Almighty and now yer swearing like a tinker."

"Mother, yer'll 'ave ter git out. Won't start now without a push." His red face was dripping with sweat as he took his jacket from Roy and threw it into the car. His passengers alighted, grumbling, and stood adrift in the dust.

Mervyn was now writhing on the grass bank, moaning softly.

"That poor boy. Where does it 'urt?" One of the ladies bent over him.

Mervyn, by way of an answer, gasped for breath.

"It's 'is backside that'll 'urt afore much longer."

"Albert, you'll 'ave to get that car started and take him to 'ospital. What say you, mother?"

Mr. Jenkinson moved a step or two towards them. Mervyn miraculously recovered his breath. "'S'alright, the wust is over. It's a-wearin' orf now."

"Then you can come an' 'elp push."

Mervyn staggered to the rear of the car. Roy felt so weak that he couldn't envisage pushing at all, but together they put their hands on the spare wheel as Mr. Jenkinson slumped into the driver's seat, still panting heavily. "Dun't you push agin the mudguards, mind," he warned.

Mervyn looked at Roy; his hands moved slowly to the edge of the vehicle.

"Right! Keep pushin' 'til she fires up! Go on!"

The slope was in their favour, and Roy barely needed to touch the car before it gained speed. His stomach ached so much he could hardly stand straight as the car's momentum carried it away. But Mervyn clung on, his hands clutching at the mudguard as he loped to keep up. Shortly, still limping, he was running. A cloud of blue smoke burst from the rear, engulfing Mervyn as the entire ensemble disappeared round the bend.

"What a brave boy. You take his bike for 'im, me dear. I s'pose we shall 'ave ter walk now 'til we catch up. Albert don't like goin' back'ards."

Roy leant on the bicycle, gradually regaining breath. The ladies picked their way down the lane until they too were lost from view. Eventually he sighed, and at last breathed normally. He wiped the tears from his cheeks, and set off with the bike.

Mervyn was sitting on a five-barred gate. "Thought you weren't a-comin'. Look." He opened his palm to reveal a sixpenny piece. "Give me a tanner, she did."

Roy handed over the bike. "I don't think it's damaged. I had a good look at it back there."

"It's me cousin's. 'E wun't care if it is, s'long as it goes.

I got summat ter show yer. Look in them stingers." He pointed to the ditch.

Roy peered, but could see nothing in particular. "What?"

Mervyn came beside him and trod down some nettles. "There."

Roy saw what looked like some kind of metal bracket, partly rusted and caked in dirt. "What's that?"

"Bit of ol' Jensey's car, that's what. 'Is mudguard'll fall orf in a bit, you see if it dun't. 'S only 'angin' on by a coupla screws. That'll come clatterin' orf 'n give 'im 'eart attack, I shun't wonder."

When they reached the village green Roy turned for home. Sunday dinner was the major family occasion of the week. But Mervyn called out, "There's summat else, 'n all."

Roy hesitated. As it was Harvest Festival, he would be expected back a little later than usual, but a further delay would be difficult to account for.

"'S alright. Wun't take a minute. Jist down the road."

A few hundred yards further, they halted just short of the brambles and again crept on to the flattened grass where Roy had crouched the previous afternoon.

"Look there."

Roy bent lower until he could see through the stems.

"By the fust tree-trunk."

Focussing on the spot, Roy made out two cats—the ginger one he'd seen yesterday, and a black one he might have remembered being stretched out on the cushions. For a moment they could, he thought, be sunning themselves, but the angle of the heads told him the truth. He wanted to be sick. He stood, then blurted, "What for? Why? What did you do that for?"

"Two seemed about the right number, Roy." Slowly, Mervyn drew a small green apple from his pocket. "One," he said, "and two," as a second followed. He pulled back his arm and hurled them together at the cottage beyond the crab-apple trees.

"One fer the sparrers and one fer the crows,
An' both of 'em up ol' Polly-Pulley's nose."

With that he scooted off, threw his leg over the crossbar and pedalled away, his laughter lingering in the noonday sunshine. Roy stepped on to the road to watch him go. Nausea made him unsteady for a moment. Then he shuddered, drew a deep breath, and headed home towards Sunday lunch.

RAINMAKER

July 1951

Roy placed the bucket at the end of the row and bent over the stalks. The leaves were yellowing but there were still plenty of green pods. He liked deciding which to pick and which to leave to fill out more. After a few minutes he was sweating. Soon his shirt clung to his back. He straightened, regarding the sky. This morning there was a wispy veil instead of the clear, sparkling blue of the last fortnight. He knew what to expect.

It didn't happen every year. Last summer was cool and wet. He'd worn a pullover most of the holidays, often carrying his raincoat. On many days he'd needed Wellington boots instead of plimsolls. But it would happen this year. Two weeks or more of glorious sunshine, cloudless skies, the grass still wet with dew in mid-morning, then dry as a bone through the long afternoons. Dry enough to sprawl headlong, wrestle and roll about—even, the other day, to doze off, thinking he was day-dreaming, then waking to find the elm trees pushing their shadows towards tea-time. But today there was this haziness, and that was how it always started.

As he worked, he recalled the sultriest summer he'd known, three years ago. Mrs. Cutler's summer. The heat had increased steadily, a whole cloudless month with barely a breeze. The haze had begun like today's. At first it had been light grey, friendly, allowing sunshine to filter through. Pleasantly warm, energising: good for running, helping in the garden, for doing errands. For two days the haze hovered, filling the horizon and thickening, changing as it did so from trouser grey to bucket grey; then a touch of blue, like a heavy dusk. Growing from the south and east, it hid the morning sun entirely. Then it became a sheet of slate, as if the sky had been tiled from the horizon to a point somewhere overhead. Where it merged with the sulphurous tinge from the brickworks to the north was an indeterminate boundary, and you could not say it was cloud, for it was formless. It was a sky without light in the morning, like dawn in the late afternoon.

He reached the end of the row, the bucket a good quarter-full. Bending made him feel faint. He noticed a few pods he'd missed, and foraging among the stalks found some pale, wrinkled ones. He'd better not take those back. He split them open, revealing peas grey with age, with white stems that had wriggled out like maggots. He threw them into the hedge. As he did so he felt how heavy his arm seemed, and again his mind went back to that sultry week, three years ago.

After days of airlessness, time had seemed irrelevant. The children sat around on the verges of dusty lanes, lolled on garden gates. Attempts at games were abandoned: rules were broken, arguments begun and tempers lost. Then they would drift home, some in tears to sulk through the evening and exasperate their exhausted mothers. They stayed up later, dreading bedtime.

For Roy, sharing a bed with his brother, there had been little sleep: sticky with sweat, tossing and turning but not admitting to being awake for fear of an argument breaking out. The hours dragged at the speed of the caterpillars that swarmed up walls and in through windows and up again across the ceiling. The cabbage-whites came from the nasturtiums near the kitchen door. They may not be squashed on the distempered walls or against the windows, so they were allowed to crawl, irrevocably, in their dozens. They sickened him. He lay in fear of them reaching the join of ceiling and wall and, finding no further surface, dropping with slimy limpness onto his head. That this had never happened didn't remove the possibility. He could imagine them in the dark, undulating across the plaster, nearing the corner, losing their grip in the struggle for more height, their rear half dangling above him, writhing... Then he would attempt to think of something else, try to remain still in the heat that blanketed everything.

Each day he had become more light-headed, almost dizzy. Everything was laborious. A few chores in the garden brought hordes of thunder-flies crawling across his scalp and under his clothes. Running brought no relief, for the air was motionless: in any case he lacked the energy. Soon even the grown-ups seemed paralysed.

One morning on his way to the shop for yet another

bottle of Tizer, he'd passed Stan the road-sweeper, characteristically leaning on his shovel.

"It'll 'ave ter rain soon. I can't stomach much more o' this," Stan complained. "I'm sweating so much jist standin' 'ere I shan't need no wash ternight. 'S all right fer you, you ain't got ter work, 'ave yer? Well, I'd better get this gutter cleared out, 'cos when it do rain we'll be a-needin' this." He stood, looking at the gully, scratching his head, and remained in that pose until the bend in the road obscured him.

By evening the sky was indigo, with an under-skin of pallid yellow from the brickfields where the chimneys' smoke could neither escape nor evaporate. There was no birdsong. Cattle were silent and motionless, except to scratch their heads against a fence-post or flick their tails at the flies. Men home from work sat in their vests on kitchen chairs in back yards or by their front doors. Their wives joined them, carrying plates of cold meals. Conversation was desultory. Wireless sets murmured unheeded in kitchens. Children slumped on moquette upholstery, fretting its patterns into their flesh, listless as the curtains at every wide-open window. Everything waited, suspended, while the sky slowly turned to charcoal.

Roy completed the second row and leant against the trunk of the nearest apple tree. Onwards, the peas were called. He wasn't sure about moving onwards: he wanted to enjoy the holidays. They would be the last before going into the top year at school. He would be working towards the eleven-plus, which might mean going to a different school from everyone else. He would stay friends, of course. But this weather made him think of unwelcome changes. He didn't know how he could stop change, or make it bearable.

On the Friday morning the sky had been black. Unable to feign sleep any longer he'd come downstairs early, even though it meant encountering his father—never at his best when getting ready for work.

"Can't you make yourself useful, instead of just sitting there?"

Roy looked round the kitchen, helplessly.

"You can put the milk bottles out before he comes. He'll be here in a minute," his mother said.

He carried out the armful of empties, arranging them in pairs on the doorstep for easy collection. Then he had gone down the garden to avoid seeing Brian. He was taking in the sweetness of the blackcurrant bushes in the dew, his nostrils among the leaves, when there was a clatter and the sound of shattering glass.

"Bugger the bloody boy!"

Roy ducked behind the bushes. He saw his father take a kick, sending a bottle across the yard where it smashed into the washhouse wall.

"No more sense than he was born with. Just wait 'til I get my hands on him!" His father grabbed his bike and hurried off round the corner.

Roy crouched in the yard, hurriedly picking up the larger pieces. He could hear the tractor slowing outside the front gate, so hid in the coal-shed until it was safe to emerge with a brush to sweep up the smaller fragments. Whilst sweeping he planned for rain. He would like to be at some distance, but he couldn't risk being caught far from home in the downpour.

The heat in the kitchen was stifling, dense as the curtains that hung over the back door in the winter to keep out the draught. What he would give for a draught... And after breakfast he had annoyed his mum by complaining about having to lift the heavy featherbed. Such a silly thing, but he wouldn't back down. He'd told her it was lumpy and that he couldn't sleep, and she'd suggested turning it over, and he'd refused because he was too hot. She'd asked if he thought he was the only one suffering, and he'd said she didn't care about him, and why couldn't his brother do it, and so it went on, out of all proportion until in the end she'd told him she could do without his help so he could take himself off, but she'd tell his father when he got home. And that on top of the broken bottle...

Roy moved his bucket along the third row and squatted for a moment. He was next to the rhubarb patch, and recalled that he'd cleared out of the house and sat out of sight under the giant leaves. He would have taken himself off to the woods, but under the pines he wouldn't see the sky darken, wouldn't even know it had started to rain until he heard thunder. No, he'd thought, he'd stay where he was. But what if the rain came that day, as he'd expected? He couldn't sit out there forever, under the umbrella leaves. And if he did, and his father came looking for him, getting wet through in the process, he'd be in even worse trouble.

He caught his arm on a half-hidden pea-stick that poked through the dry leaves. He tugged at the stick but it was clamped so firmly by the clay that it snapped off. In the stillness the sound seemed loud, as if a thick branch had been struck by lightning. He knew about lightning.

There was a shattered stump in a row of oak trees along Honeypot Lane. The tree had been struck before he was born, but its blackened skeleton still haunted that stretch. And worse, when he was four, two farm-workers had been killed as they sheltered under a tree. That was during the war, when the thunder was so noisy his parents had looked south to see if the sky was red in case the Blitz had re-started. He'd heard aeroplanes overhead that year, but it wasn't the Blitz: it was, he later learned, the raids on Coventry to the north-west. He could remember the awful sound of the air-raid sirens, too, that sent him flying downstairs to his parents, claiming they had said he could hear some comedy show or other on the wireless. They let him stay up until the all-clear sounded.

And only last year Dotty Parker had been struck by lightning as she was washing up at her kitchen sink. Lightning had snaked through her open window and burnt her hands. He could still see her white face as she was brought from across the road into the church hall where the children were having dinner. She sat huddled in a blanket in the corner. The children were told not to stare but to eat their dark, wet cabbage: so, they did, even swallowing the thick stalks which they normally left, rather than be caught peering at her. When they were marched back to school in their crocodile, they whispered to each other.

"Did you see 'er?"

"No."

"She went all purple."

"No she din't. She were blue."

"'Ow d'yer know if yer din't see 'er?"

He never understood how anyone knew she had been hit. She was on her own in the house, struck dumb by the flash. Could she have walked by herself? Did the lightning make some kind of ripping noise as it seared her flesh, so that the dinner ladies heard it even as they were ladling out the greens?

But in Mrs. Cutler's summer, three years ago, when that storm finally unleashed itself in a fury of gales, the chimney-stack collapsed through her cottage roof. It had pinned the elderly woman to her bed. All kinds of rumour swept along the houses. He'd been told not to go near. But he did, the next morning, in a gap between the squalls. He'd gawped at the smashed roof and tumbled brickwork. Two men swayed on ladders in the wind, stretching canvas over a ragged hole in the slates.

Stan was there in his official capacity, shovelling old mortar and bits of brick into a wheelbarrow. "Could o' killed 'er, that," he observed, pausing to lean on his shovel. "Made 'er stay in bed, anyways. Kept 'er out o' my way. She'd be naggin' at me ter stake up 'er roses if she were a-watchin' me." Roy imagined a workman peering down at her and she looking up at the tarpaulin flapping around his head like the wings of the Angel of Death.

That autumn Mrs. Cutler died. Some said she would have reached a hundred but for the shock of that chimney. Others thought the heat had done for her, as she'd already taken to her bed. Stan reckoned, "She would a-died afore long, sooner or later. We all on us do."

Roy began to pick the final row. The bucket was over half-full. He had far more than they'd need for tonight, but he was certain it would rain and that he wouldn't be able to tread on the soil again for at least a couple of days. But then, in Mrs. Cutler's summer he had expected rain for a whole week before it arrived. He thought again of that Friday. It was much darker than when there'd been a partial eclipse. It was surely upon them: it had to rain before the day was out. Everyone would go mad if not. The sky was threatening fire and brimstone. He had crept out from under the rhubarb, sticky and cramped, shivering despite the heat.

You were supposed to believe in God to escape the wrath of the heavens. He went to church every week: he knew his prayers by heart. But believing in God was difficult, and he didn't know if he really believed, or if behaving as if he did, especially on Sundays, was actually believing. Lots of the children avoided church now, even though several had previously sung in the choir, and he was often teased for having continued to do so. So, he didn't think much about God on weekdays, except when he was afraid. And he'd been afraid then—scared of the lightning that would shred the sky and the terrible, overlapping thunder that would crash inside his head. He was sorry he'd lost his temper, and hoped his mother would forgive him. And he was afraid of what his father would do when he came home if she didn't, so he'd crept back under the rhubarb and made up a prayer for rain.

And while he prayed, he'd imagined the first heavy drops: how you'd snatch washing off the line, bundling it anyhow to get it inside, and how you lugged the bikes into the barn. How you stood out in it, taking your shirt off to feel the moisture on your skin. How you would try to drink it, head thrown back, water trickling down your face, your shoulders glistening with the slippery mix of sweat and rain. How scents rose from the grass, how leaves shed rivulets of dust with each impact. How you were called to your senses and must rush inside to close the windows, then dash out again to take the lid off the water butt and shove buckets under the down pipes. How the drains gurgled, and the rain hissed and bounced off the ground. How you dodged inside as the first lightning licked the skyline, and how all the time there was a crescendo until thunder drummed and thrashed in your ears to the exclusion of all other sound.

He had slid out from the rhubarb, imagining his prayer rising towards God and piercing the bottom of the cloud. He'd seen the base of the blackness overhead sagging, ragged with the weight of water, just as Mrs. Cutler's tarpaulin had sagged when the heavens opened again after the workmen had finished. He'd dragged his feet along the path, thinking of how his mother wouldn't speak to him at dinnertime. He was wondering what he could say to make up, when there was a soft thud. He peered at the ground. At the edge of one of the half-inch cracks was a dark patch, spreading a little and soaking into the earth. And he was overwhelmed with relief, for he knew his bad behaviour would be forgotten...

He picked up the bucket and moved it to the end of the row. This wasn't going to compare with those violent storms he'd been recalling. This was just a storm in a teacup, in a bucket. He might never witness another like Mrs. Cutler's unless, when older, he went to the tropics. But there they had snakes, giant ants and poisonous spiders creeping about inside their straw huts. He wouldn't like that.

The old villagers still insisted that there'd been worse storms than Mrs. Cutler's. During the First World War, they said, and another like it in the twenties. He hadn't believed them, and still couldn't. But three years ago, just about here, where he now stood on the garden path, he had been thoroughly convinced of the existence of God. But that was then, when he was only eight: he was older now, and, he reckoned, much, much wiser.

NOTHING BUT THE SUN

July 1952

The final summer. Even with the windows flung open, the classroom was stifling, and Miss Burton daily more irritable. The five top year pupils had finished schoolwork. The eleven-plus had been their ultimate test. The others accepted their results with philosophical fortitude, whereas Roy's sense of achievement was tarnished by the prospect of upheaval. To distract himself he suggested that they put on a play for the end of the year. Miss Burton gave cautious approval, with warnings about behaviour. She wouldn't allow rehearsals out of class until the morning of the performance, on the penultimate day of term. Roy would have to organise the others at playtimes and dinnertimes. And what was the play, exactly?

"It's one I've written," he answered. "It's not too long. A boy goes into the village shop and steals something. I don't know what, yet. Perhaps sweets. He tells his friend. The friend won't eat any and says they should be put back. They argue, but in the end the first boy returns them."

"That's very good. Are there other parts?"

Roy hesitated. The idea wasn't his, but came from a story he'd read. It had only three characters. He needed five. "The shopkeeper, another customer, and the second boy's mother, because she tells him what to say to the first boy."

"Wouldn't he have eaten them by then?"

That night he sat up in bed, working out a dramatised version. It was too hot to sleep. As he tired, he found he was merely copying the original, and had to rewrite much of it. This time he considered the problem Miss Burton had identified, and realised that the action needed to happen in one place. Could the second boy wait outside the shop, on one side of the stage? The mother could be the other customer, so that she was on hand. But then a grown-up would do something about the theft there and then, not discuss it. And this would reduce the parts, leaving someone in the group with nothing to do. Or there would be a second customer with nothing to say. He removed the second boy's mother altogether, deciding instead on the original customer, accompanied by her daughter. (He'd find a way of bringing her into the dialogue later.) He scrawled in pencil across the pages, barely legibly. He found it hard to leave things out of the original, and when he finished he still had no lines for the little girl.

Derek, of course, was to be the villain. "Shan't do it, else," he threatened. "An' s'pose you'll be the goody-goody."

Mervyn was the shopkeeper. Roy dissuaded him

from stealing props from the village shop. "We'll make do with empty tins and boxes. We can all collect some."

"I en't 'avin nuffin' ter do wiv it," Rose pronounced, planting her arms firmly across her chest. "Shan't come ter school anyway, last few days. Waste o' time. Me cousin'll 'ave 'ad 'er second by then, so I'll be busy 'elpin' 'er. Daphne can do it instead o' me."

"She can't. She's not in our year group."

"Wha's it matter?"

So Daphne agreed to be the customer with Joan, being tiny, as her daughter.

At the first reading, a morning playtime, Roy told them the story, suggesting they read it through. Joan said she needed to go to the lavatory. Roy said that was all right because she hadn't any lines.

"What 'm I s'posed to do, then?" she asked.

"Listen to us read it. You can think of things to say as we go along."

"Don't sound like it matters much, then, do it?" she pouted. She slouched off, dragging her feet over the tarmac.

Derek called after her. "'Course it dun't matter. Yer only a girl."

Joan turned to answer him, but was knocked over by a girl playing hopscotch.

Derek fell about. "Did yer see that?" he guffawed.

"Come on," said Roy, "we've only got a few minutes."

They made a start, heads clumped together.

"Ain't yer got no more copies?" asked Daphne. "Me neck's achin' already."

"Can't read this anyway," Derek complained. "It's scribble."

"Don't need ter," Mervyn decided. "Le's jist make it up."

"All right," sighed Roy. "You know how it starts. Let's act it out. Mervyn, you stand there, behind your counter."

"Where's all the money?"

"Have a box in front of you."

"How much'd be in it? Five pounds?"

"If you like."

"Cor! I'm rich then."

"Daphne, you come in."

"Where's the door?"

"Doesn't matter yet. Oh, all right, use the gate."

She opened the gate and stepped through.

Miss Burton appeared from nowhere. "You're not to go out of the yard at play-time, Daphne. You know that."

"Please Miss—" Roy began, but she was already shepherding Daphne back. "Time for the whistle, anyway," she added, giving a shrill blast.

Derek, usually the last in line, sprang to his feet, treading on the script, and ran to form the queue at the door.

Rehearsals, if such they could be called, went on in this way until Mervyn was absent for several days. Roy said they should use the time to learn their lines, but Joan pointed out that she had none, and it wasn't her job to think any up.

"Jist act like a baby, like y'always do," said Derek.

"Stop it, Derek. Let's practice our scene. Don't just stand there gormlessly, argue with me about not taking them back."

Derek abandoned speech altogether and started a wrestling match.

"You can't just fight," said Roy, pulling free.

"Well, I ain't got nothin' to put back, 'ave I? Can't yer pinch summat from yer Grandad's shop?"

Daphne volunteered to prompt Derek, who woodenly repeated each word.

"How c'n we do the end when you ain't done the beginnin'?" Joan protested.

By the end of the second week, they were all tired of it. Roy had written out another copy, with some lines for Joan, but these were repeatedly drowned by Mervyn or Derek, who took little notice of the script. Roy went to Miss Burton to voice doubts about the project, but she had informed the school governors of the performance. "And after all, Roy," she reminded him, "it was you who suggested it. And could you tidy up that pile of boxes in the cloakroom? I'm sure you don't need so many. The little ones can't reach their pegs."

At last came the big day. The final rehearsal showed some sign of progress. There was now a reliable pattern to some sections. It began firmly with Mervyn and Daphne, with Derek convincing as the thief. But they hadn't reached the end of the piece, and Joan had given up trying to squeeze her three lines in. However, Daphne had the idea of emerging from the shop and hearing Derek brag about the sweets, then supporting Roy in telling him to return them. If Derek did so, straight away, she would say nothing. She would give Roy a threepenny bit so he could buy sweets to distract Mr. Sullivan, giving Derek ample time to replace the goods. "That's brilliant!" Roy enthused. "You're really clever, Daphne."

At dinnertime the three boys pushed the desks back and rearranged the chairs. Boxes of tins and cartons were stacked beside two desks serving as the counter. Through the open window Roy heard the whistle, and Miss Burton insisting on silence in the line. "Now children," she began, "this afternoon we've something different from our usual lessons…"

He felt sick. Why had he started this? It was the stupidest thing he'd ever done. He needed his brains testing. Mervyn and Derek seemed unconcerned, piling tins onto the counter. The younger children entered the room in a state of high excitement. Most had never seen a play. They clamoured, despite Miss Burton's stern presence, clambering over the unfamiliar rows of chairs. She blew the whistle once more. "If I have to blow this whistle again, the play will not be performed." Please, thought Roy, please! But there was silence. "Some of the older children have been working hard to put their play on for you. You must listen carefully, because the play has a very important message for all of us. You mustn't interrupt them, but you may clap at the end. I will not call the register this afternoon, I will simply fill it in. I can see you all perfectly well from here." She sat on her high chair, moved this once to the side, from where she gazed around. "You may begin."

Mervyn took his position behind the counter. He picked up two tins and changed them over. He took out a dirty handkerchief and dusted the counter. He adjusted other tins, turning their labels to the front. He was absorbed in these actions, and totally credible, his grubbiness apart. The little ones at the front, sitting on cushions, began to fidget. Mervyn walked towards them.

"Them mice've bin at the cheese agin," he announced. Somebody tittered. Miss Burton looked up sharply. "I wonder 'oo'll be my first customer today?" he went on. "Roll up, roll up! Fifty pounds I've taken this week already. Fifty pounds! What d'yer think o' that?"

Roy, despite himself, was enthralled. He noticed the teacher, pen forgotten in her hand as she watched. Mervyn was so natural—none of this had existed until this moment. Things would turn out for the better after all. He realised that Mervyn had forgotten his opening line, which was Daphne's cue, but somehow it didn't matter. Daphne too was entranced, watching from the opposite side, Joan and Derek beside her.

Mervyn was bending behind the counter now. He reappeared with a brush and dustpan, evidently taken from the cloakroom. "Sweep them droppings up," he said, approaching the little ones once more. Laughter again. Miss Burton half stood, glaring at the miscreants.

Roy caught Daphne's eye across the room. He raised

his eyebrows and tilted his head. She took the hint and entered. "Mornin' Mr. Sullivan," she called, shopping basket at the ready, and looking grown-up in her mother's hat. Joan trotted on behind her.

"Ah, there you are!" exclaimed Mervyn. "Thought I weren't goin' ter see yer today Missus—er—Missus."

There was more giggling, but Daphne wasn't put off. She made a remark about the weather and gave her order to perfection.

Mervyn, improvising still, asked her if she would like "a nice bit o' that there cheddar."

"No!" squealed one of the little ones. "It's 'ad mice in it!"

There was an outburst of laughter.

"No it ain't," Mervyn said accusingly to the front row.

"It 'as, it 'as!"

The audience entered fully into the debate. Miss Burton strode onto the stage and blew her whistle. She gave a final warning, but there was an air of excitement now.

The play resumed. Roy felt the energy: he was transfixed. This was so much better than he had dared hope, even if the lines were all over the place. Daphne kept the story going despite everything, neatly cueing in Derek, then resuming her conversation with Mervyn.

Derek had turned his jacket collar up and peered furtively over it, crossing the stage in elongated strides. He opened a box and brought out two packets of cigarettes, stuffing them into his pockets. Roy was aghast. The whistle blew. Miss Burton demanded, "Where have those come from?"

"They're me dad's, Miss."

"I see. I thought you said sweets, Roy?"

He thought quickly. "I said they could be those sweet cigarettes, Miss. Derek perhaps didn't hear me properly."

"Hmm. I'll take those. Give them to me." She put down her whistle and took the packets.

"I gotta 'ave summat," Derek complained.

"I've some chocolate 'e can use, Miss," said Daphne, going to the bag that had contained the hat and producing half a Mars bar.

"Mmmm!" went the little ones.

"Now carry on. You're doing very well, but perhaps you should bring it to an end soon." Miss Burton marched back, but remained standing.

Daphne picked up the dialogue while Derek placed the Mars bar, retreated in his strange stride, then advanced again to steal it back.

Joan piped up. "I want a wee-wee. Mum, I want a wee." There was a fit of giggles.

"Be quiet, Sally," said Daphne. "We're going home in a minute."

"I do though. I want one, really." She turned her knees inward, clenching her thighs. The audience was whispering. Someone cackled. Derek approached Roy, who stepped forward to greet him. There was a groan from Joan.

Daphne said, "I'd better take you 'ome then. Quick! Goodbye Mr. Sullivan," and rushed Joan out of the room.

Roy felt his knees weaken. It dawned on him that Joan's need was real, which is why she had spoken for the first time with conviction. With Daphne having gone there was nobody for him to consult. He too would have to improvise.

Derek rushed into his speech, brandishing the chocolate, before Roy could collect himself. He was racking his brains as to how to persuade Derek to part with his trophy when the whistle blew. He looked up and saw Mervyn, armed with Miss Burton's whistle, advancing sternly towards them.

"Now then, young varmint. I knows what you's up to. Turn yer pockets out. Wha's this you got 'ere? You's a-comin' down to the station, you young rascal."

Mervyn to the rescue! Nobody could doubt he was the local bobby. He had P.C. Anderson's voice, his stance, and seemed almost to have his stature. The play would end on an unprepared but highly satisfactory note.

Then, beyond the two boys Roy saw Miss Burton approaching, red in the face with fury. He moved between her and his actors to forestall her.

"You come along o' me."

"No I wun't!" shouted Derek, falling on Mervyn. The two wrestled each other for a moment before stumbling to the floor. Miss Burton couldn't get near: their boots and fists were flying in all directions. The audience leapt up and down, "Fight! Fight!"

A cheer went up as the stack of boxes collapsed, tins rattling and rolling about the floor.

"Fight! Fight! Fight!"

He never knew the sequel. He slipped out of the room. Daphne was in the cloakroom, wringing out Joan's knickers. Joan, white-faced, sat blubbing on a bench. Daphne indicated the classroom, where the pandemonium was increasing. "I'm sorry. She felt sick, din't yer Joan? I couldn't let 'er go 'ome by 'erself, could I? She weren't old enough."

It took a moment for either of them to realise what she had said.

"It's all right. You were brilliant. So was Mervyn."

"'Ow did it finish?"

"I don't think it's ended yet." Roy moved down the corridor. "Come on," he said, taking a step towards the outside door.

"It's nowhere near 'ome time."

"Doesn't matter. She won't notice."

"I'm waiting for me sister," said Joan.

"I'll jist get me mum's 'at. I'll catch yer up," promised Daphne.

He wouldn't come to school tomorrow. He'd be ill. He wouldn't speak again to Miss Burton. Mervyn he might see in the holidays, knocking about the village, and he supposed he wouldn't be able to avoid Derek.

He'd begun his schooldays, aged four, with a sulk.

He'd refused to speak to anyone because he believed he should have been five before he started. He'd held out for almost a week, not saying a word. Now he was leaving in another silence, without farewells.

He went through the school gateway for the last time, and waited until Daphne arrived, clutching the hat. "The bag dun't matter, but I bet I wun't see that Mars bar agin." She chuckled. "They'm still fightin', 'n Miss is yellin' an' screamin' at 'em."

They dawdled in the shade of the beeches, then drifted off through the fields, away from the village. He knew they could fill the afternoon exactly as they wished, that for an hour or so nothing but the sun could touch them.

NOT CRICKET

August 1952

The first few weeks of the summer holidays had been cloudy and cool. When the weather warmed the air grew humid. One night, covered in sweat, the sheets clinging to his legs, Roy was woken by explosions of thunder. The room was pierced by lightning. He worried that the sycamore at the bottom of the garden would be struck. He counted the intervals between the lightning and the thunderclaps, and as these increased and the storm rumbled into the distance he fell into a doze. He woke to a sunrise that at last promised the weather for which he and all the children had been waiting.

The skies cleared, each morning's dew quickly burning off. Pullovers and cardigans were abandoned and, as the puddles dried, plimsolls and sandals replaced shoes and wellingtons. Attics and cupboards under the stairs were deserted, leaving jumbles of dolls, crayons, colouring books, Meccano and Plasticine. The children hiked and rampaged and shrieked and shouted from one end of the village to the other. They shimmied through the woods, dived into hedges, tumbled down grassy banks and rolled among the ferns; they crawled along the drying ditches and tore over barbed wire fences; they flattened dens in the cornfields and crept into corners of forbidden orchards. Straw and twigs threaded their hair, grass and leaves dried in the smalls of their backs and the creases of their stomachs. They were stung, scratched, grazed and bruised; their bodies glowed like copper. They hurtled through the heat of the day and wove into the evening mists, when twilight wiped the dust from their eyes and their pupils shone back at the rising moon. They played every outdoor game they could think of, and when their collective memory was exhausted, they invented new adventures.

Virtually every child in the village took part in this festival, quirky, unpredictable and absorbing as it was. Anything that threatened to keep a child away was circumnavigated: it would slip away before the morning bus was due for the planned shopping trip; it would forget that Auntie and Uncle were travelling from Bedford to visit in the afternoon, and it would complete the usually long-drawn-out chores in the twinkle of an eye. So, it endured for ten days or so. Then exhaustion set in: play led to dispute, conversation to argument, teasing to name-calling, banter to fighting. The younger children tended not to appear after dinner-time, preferring the cool of indoors. They were nuisances to mothers. "Why can't you go out to play, weather like this? I don't know what to do with you for the life of me."

For the older ones, afternoons were oases where leaves hung limp and dust lay undisturbed. A desultory ramble would be terminated beyond the last cottage on whichever lane they followed. Once they took a communal picnic intended for consumption in the pine forest of the next parish, but for some it was too tempting and for all it was too bothersome to carry, so they flopped down on the village green and, despite their recent dinners, polished it off before two o'clock.

Towards the end of the second week of the heat wave, even their numbers dwindled. Mick was, he claimed, ensnared by shopping. Pauline was unprecedentedly in demand to look after her sister. Alan withdrew with a headache, or stomach-ache, or hay fever. Joan's bladder condition had always meant her excursions were brief, but now she was rarely seen beyond the shade of her front porch.

The remainder sprawled under the elms alongside the playing field. They chewed stems of grass, to the drone of insects or subdued staccato of yellowhammers in the hedge. They were still for long periods, unusually quiet. Derek would now and then throw out a challenge—a wrestling match, a throwing competition, a race to the swings and back. The girls ignored him, though Daphne once unexpectedly leapt up and sprinted towards the swings. Derek, slow to react, lumbered after, complaining about a false start. But she ran twice round the swings instead of the single obligatory circuit, ensuring he overtook her, thus avoiding a wrangle over alleged cheating or a second "proper" contest. Nobody had the energy for either.

Rose told Daphne about her sister's engagement, how she'd fallen in love. Roy lay back in the shade, gazing at the deep blue overhead, featureless and infinite. He tried to remember other summers, but even the memories of a few weeks ago belonged to another existence. He recalled wan sunlight glistening on the wet window of the front room as he sat reading or listening to the wireless. Last year the holidays had been spent in a loft in one of Grandad's barns, where he and Derek had formed a succession of secret societies. Each was inaugurated with a purpose, but after the rules of membership had been formulated (always the same ones), would become ill-defined. It amounted to little more than sitting like hens in a coop, hardly able to manoeuvre round each other without banging heads or balancing precariously on the main support beam. The only thrill was in defying his grandad's orders not to go up there in the first place. Grandad was either taking an after-dinner nap, pottering in the garden or, occasionally, trudging to his grocery shop by the front gate to serve a customer. He was, therefore, oblivious to their disobedience, so there was little satisfaction in the escapade. That kind of thing was best left for winter anyway, when darkness and the lighting of a candle increased the risk.

But there had been one memorable summer, the first after he started school. His mother was in hospital for three weeks for an operation. He remembered his father doing housework or thrashing at the garden path with a sickle before cycling off to work at half-past six. One morning Roy had been woken by a shout of "Blast it! Bugger the bloody bucket!" followed by a rolling, clanking, then the creak of the bike-chain and the slam of the gate.

Each day he washed up, made his bed and tidied. He was always at home when his father returned, tired and ill-tempered, but, except on one occasion when he was taken to visit his pale mother, he escaped outside again as soon as he could. Sundays were the worst. His dad tried to cook the traditional Sunday lunch to maintain normality. Those were dinners of cindered Yorkshire pudding, burnt gravy and charred greens: everything scorched, as if the world was on fire.

But what he recollected most about those weeks was Daphne's Auntie Jean. She lived nearby and, having recently left school, was waiting to start work as a secretary. Sometimes Roy had meals at her house with her and her mum, who smelt of carbolic, but more often they took a picnic to the woods, sometimes with Daphne, though she says she can't remember much. He'd missed his mum, but once he knew she was getting better he didn't worry any more.

Daphne's Auntie Jean taught him games and told him stories. Some she made up; others were about people in the village in what she called the olden days, about which she had herself been told. Some were sad episodes: a young woman drowning under the ice on Hatter's Pond, or a boy hanging himself in what was now Jenkinson's hay barn. She told him how, just before she was born, half the village had gone up on the ridge to watch the airship. Her mum said it was a real effort for her to walk up there, expecting as she was. And it was a shock when the huge craft only just cleared the treetops. Old Ted Maundsley said he'd eat his hat if it got to India. When the story had been retold Daphne's Auntie Jean wondered what his hat would have tasted like, but later she learnt he hadn't had to eat it after all.

She told of the deepest snow-drifts anyone could remember, with the village cut off for a fortnight and the men of the parish being called out with shovels, and how the first route to be cleared stopped at the Ploughman's. She described a cricket match where his own father, hurrying to an away game after work one Saturday lunchtime, snatched a nightdress from the drawer instead of his cricket shirt, but had to wear it anyway, and how, in the same match, Limpy Dimble tired of chasing to the boundary and brought his bike onto the field to save his legs. She had also seen her uncle cram the football team into his Austin Seven, except for the captain who had to follow on his bike. And it was Daphne's Auntie Jean who said he needn't be afraid of Old Jacob, who tramped for miles but always took the same course through the villages, turning up at the same time each year.

And Daphne's Auntie Jean searched for mushrooms, or found a wren's nest, or explained where the biggest chestnuts would fall in a few weeks' time. Sometimes they went up to Jensey's field and fed carrots to two shire horses grazing there, the bulk of their working days behind them. Roy, through all this companionship, couldn't describe how happy he felt deep inside. Deep as the sky above him now.

"I want it always to be like this," he murmured.

"Like what?" asked Derek.

"This. Summer, hot. Lying here on the grass, bone dry."

"Be borin'."

"I'd never get bored. Wish every summer was like it. I never want it to end."

"Wait 'til school starts agin. It'll 'ave ended then all right."

Roy was the first from the village to have passed the eleven-plus in four years. He would not be moving to the secondary modern with the rest: Derek, Mervyn, Rose and Joan. "Yer'll git longer 'olidays than us," Derek jibed. "Them cocky buggers don't 'ave ter start when us ordin'ry folk do."

"'Ave yer got yer uniform yit?" asked Daphne.

"No. Next week." This was a lie, but it couldn't be proven.

"You'm be a posh-at," jeered Rose.

"We only 'as ter git a tie. We en't posh. We dun't walk about swankin,'" Derek taunted.

"Y'en't got nuffin' ter swank about," said Daphne. She quickly continued. "Wish I were clever. Mind you I wun't want to wear that 'Igh School git-up. They all look like ol' maids ter me. Still, I 'opes I passes when it's my turn."

For a moment they pondered the unvisited corridors of academia.

"Snobs," concluded Derek. "'Ole bloody lot ov 'em. Stuck-up snobs."

"I'm not a snob!" Roy rose to the bait despite himself.

"Yer talk like one though. I bet yer in two years' time yer wun't 'ave nuffin' ter do wiv us lot."

"Bet I will then."

"Yer'll see."

Roy didn't want to anticipate two weeks ahead, never mind two years.

"I'll see you each week, anyway. In the choir."

"Wish I din't 'ave ter go no more," Derek announced. "It's fer cissies. Anyway, singin's soppy."

Daphne said, "I like singin'. I go 'cos've the choir."

"Never even wanted ter go ter Sunday School. 'Ated it."

"I din't go ter church at all when I were little, 'cept fer Auntie Jean's funeral." She started to make a daisy-chain. There was silence except for the hum of a bee that nobody tried to waft away.

Roy saw the hearse in the spring sunshine: beyond it, primroses on the verge, and above the hedge lapwings flopping in the brisk wind. He shivered, despite the heat. Rising on an elbow, he turned to Daphne, but did not meet her eye. He rolled out of the tree's shade, feeling warmth surge over him. In or beyond that ice-cold blue was Daphne's Auntie Jean. The blue that went on forever.

Rose started to tell Daphne about her sister's pregnancy. Derek did a backward roll, finishing alongside Roy. "Game o' cricket?"

Roy surveyed the group. "There's only four of us." Sam and William, notoriously uncoordinated, looked shiftily at each other. Roy had seen William hit himself on the head when batting, and knew that whatever selection system was used, he would have William in his team. But he wouldn't invite another accusation of snobbery. "Okay. If the girls will play. There'd be four fielders then." There would be a chance of fair play if Daphne was on his side.

"All right," Rose conceded, "but tomorrer you got ter play mothers and fathers. That's fair. 'N I'm married ter Derek, 'n Daphne and Roy can live next door 'n I've got two babies and them's Sam and Will."

Roy lay back and closed his eyes. There'd be no cricket now.

"All right, only I aint farm-workin'. I'm in a factory making summat wiv machines."

Roy sat upright. He stared at Derek in disbelief. 'Mothers and fathers' was for the nippers. They'd last played it at Easter. Derek had bossed the little ones about so much that one of them ran home crying. He and Derek had decided that the game was too babyish. He looked round at the faces: Rose, Daphne, the two boys. They seemed to find the arrangement unremarkable.

"Go orn then," Derek said. "Don't jist sit there. Go 'n get yer bat. Mine's busted."

"Don't git an 'ard ball, neiver," added Rose. "I ain't playin' wiv no 'ard 'n."

Slowly, Roy stood up. He glared again at Derek, who was unflinching. "Right," he said, "you can pick sides while I'm gone."

He dawdled home, easing the inertia from his legs. He

searched under the stairs for a tennis ball and collected his bat from the shed. They could argue over selection before he returned. He found it hard to shake the afternoon's lethargy. The heat beat back into his face from the road and there was a heavy droning in his head. On returning he found the others calm: there seemed to have been no dispute.

"Yer bin ages," Derek complained.

"Couldn't find a good ball," Roy lied—for the second time that afternoon, he realised.

"We've picked sides. Yer've got Sam 'n Will."

Sam looked at Roy with an expression that combined apology with apprehension. Will picked up the bat and swung round and round until dizziness caused him to topple over Rose's spread-eagled legs.

"Git orf, Will! That 'urt!" She slapped his shoulder until he rolled off, whimpering.

Roy considered his team. "It's a bit one-sided."

"What you complainin' about, Roy Newsome?" Rose thrust her face at him. "You lot've got three boys."

"Le's get on wiv it. We're battin' first. Bags I'm Dennis Compton." Derek snatched the bat from Will and marched towards the roller that would act as stumps.

"'S only a game," Daphne said quietly, passing Roy as he prepared to bowl.

With so few fielders Derek could risk slogging. Sam and Will chased eagerly to begin with, but before long they were merely trotting, and Roy had to do more of the fielding. Daphne ran keenly and threw in strongly, but Rose sauntered, and only then if the ball was so near her that nobody else moved. She threw as limply as Will, the ball coming to rest in the long grass well short of its supposed destination. When the ball beat the bat, wicketkeeper Sam would also miss, allowing Derek to run byes. "We can't have extras," Roy protested, coming down the pitch to pick up yet another abandoned ball.

"Can. I bin runnin' em since we started."

"But Sam can't stop anything and Rose won't cover him. It would be better if Daphne kept wicket."

"Can't bowl or keep wicket fer the other side."

"'Oo sez I can't run?" Rose piped up.

"I didn't say you couldn't. I said you won't. You're not even trying."

"I am, see. But me leg 'urts where Will landed on me. Yours'd 'urt if e'd clumped a bat on your legs."

Roy sighed. His next delivery caught the shoulder of the bat and lifted vertically over Sam. The keeper ran in circles under it, arms outstretched.

"Catch it!" Roy shouted.

Sam retreated in a wide arc, gaping upwards. The ball fell to earth behind him as Derek completed his run.

Rose strolled across and handed the ball to Sam. "'Ere it is. 'Ard luck."

Derek began a second run.

"Hang on," Roy said. "You can't take another, the ball's dead."

"Wha's it died of?" squealed Rose.

"Hit the roller, Sam. Run him out!" called Roy as Derek elbowed past him.

Sam took aim, but Rose stood in front of him so that he couldn't throw, and Derek reached safety.

"That's not fair! The ball was dead. Sam's the wicket-keeper and it was in his hands."

"'E weren't nowhere near the wicket, though, were 'e? 'E were more like longstop when 'e got it. Anyway, if it were dead why did yer yell at 'im to throw at the stumps? I wun't o' bin out if 'e'd 'it'em, would I? So there."

"He didn't hit them 'cos she stood in the way."

"Yer said I wun't move, so I come to 'elp Sam. 'N 'oo's she—the cat's mother?"

The drone in Roy's head had become a low throb. Confronted, he capitulated. "Stay close to the roller, Sam."

"But yer said to catch it."

Roy sighed again. He might as well take them all on. Daphne came across. "'Ow many yer got, Derek?"

Roy interjected, "Thirty-six."

"Thirty-seven wiv them two."

"Ain't that enuff?"

"I'll declare at fifty, then you two can 'ave yer innin's."

"We'll git fifty-two then." She laughed. "Come on Roy, give 'im easy ones so's 'e'll git there quicker."

But Roy determined to thwart the half-century. He thundered off, bowling faster with each delivery. One reared off a tussock and hit Sam in the face. The fielders gathered round him. The captains glared at each other down the pitch.

"'E's all right now," said Rose, drying his tears with her hankie. "If it still 'urts tomorrer I'll kiss it better when I'm yer mum. If it gets wuss we'll go ter the doctor's." The girls took up their positions, but Will stayed alongside Sam.

Derek stroked the next ball gently to where Will had been fielding. Roy started off to gather it, but Daphne raced in and collected it instead. Her throw came in hard, narrowly missing Derek's head. Roy was encouraged.

On forty-three Derek swung to leg and missed, the ball thudding into his calf.

"How's that? Leg before!"

"Never!" Derek stepped to the side and rubbed his thigh. "It were a quick 'un though."

"Plumb in front."

"It were goin' over the top."

"It didn't hit you there. It whacked you on the shin."

"I can feel where it 'it me. I dun't need tellin' be you."

Roy looked at the others. Will was examining Sam's reddening eye. Rose was tying her shoelace. He turned to Daphne.

"It were low," she said.

Derek looked as if he could hit her with the bat. Then he tilted his head to one side, fixing on Roy. "It were a no-ball."

"It was what?" said Roy, incredulous.

"Yer bent yer arm. It were a throw. Weren't a proper bowl. No ball." Derek returned to the crease and took up his stance. "Ready," he said, tapping his bat professionally. Roy glanced towards Daphne, but she had turned round and was sitting down, facing away from the pitch.

"Daphne, was it a throw?"

"Dun't know the difference. Let 'im git 'is fifty 'n git it over wiv."

Roy stalked down the pitch, heart thumping, eyes stinging with sweat. The pounding in his head was deafening.

Derek straightened, swinging the bat malevolently. "Bowl then."

Roy approached him, paused, then continued past, handing the ball to Will. "Your turn."

"'E can't bowl!" exclaimed Derek.

"He can. He's on my side."

"But 'e dun't know 'ow!"

"We'll have to help him then. Come on, Will." He led him to the other end of the pitch. "Aim with your left arm and swing your right one over."

Will's first attempt bounced in front of him and rolled three yards down the pitch.

"No ball!" claimed Derek.

Roy agreed. "That's one more to you then. Try a little run-up. It might go further."

Will trotted up, flung his arm over, but forgot to release the ball, throwing himself to the ground.

"No ball!"

"It's not a run. He didn't let go. He didn't bowl anything."

Derek fumed: Roy knew he wanted to reach his fifty

with a six. Another delivery trickled halfway down the pitch.

"One more on the score," allowed Roy.

And so it continued, Derek inching to his half-century without his bat making further contact.

The game moved on quickly. The girls added three runs to the total, then Roy's side went in. Will was bowled first ball. Sam said he still couldn't see properly so wouldn't bat. Roy had regained energy since he'd finished bowling, though the drumming sensation intensified. He managed to connect some hearty swipes and soon reached twenty. Derek became serious in his captaincy. He spoke sharply to Rose when once she misfielded. She sulked and stood behind the wicket with folded arms. Shortly after, Roy edged the ball past her. It should have been caught but he took a single instead. Twenty-eight. He managed, by springing out of the crease and swinging wildly, to send one ball into the wheat field for a six. Will and Daphne took several minutes to find it, while Sam said he'd have to go home and rinse out his eye. Derek was now crazed. He strode fully twenty yards on his run-up and charged down the pitch after each delivery. He pursued the ball if Roy missed it, finishing up beyond Rose, still standing with her arms across her chest. When Roy made contact, Derek wheeled and pivoted, leapt and sprinted in pursuit, spraying sweat in all directions.

Thirty-seven. Roy's eye was in. He was middling almost every ball now as Derek's bowling grew ragged. Rose said, "Why dun't yer let Daphne bowl?"

Derek, breath rasping, stood with hands on his knees and glared at her. "Girls can't."

"Well git 'im out if yer so good, 'cos it's getting' on fer tea-time 'n I'm goin' in a minute."

Derek regarded her with disdain.

There was going to be such a row the girls would withdraw and Will, terrified, would follow Sam home. Then any runs Roy scored wouldn't count because of the absence of fielders. Instead, to Roy's surprise, Derek turned back to begin his run-up. Roy settled in the crease. The next delivery was the quickest he had received. All of Derek's strength went into it, but it was over-pitched. Full toss! Roy threw himself into the stroke. The ball smacked resoundingly off the bat and flew towards Daphne. It was certain to be a boundary, but he started to run to be on the safe side. Daphne jabbed out a hand: the ball stuck as her fingers closed round it. She held her arm out, staring at the ball in astonishment. Then she let it fall to the ground.

"What a catch!" Derek was beside himself. "Smashin' bit o' fieldin'. Smashin'!"

"I dropped it," she said, looking down at the ball.

"Y'eld on ter it long enuff. Wha' a catch!" Derek walked towards Rose. "I knew if I bowled 'im a full toss 'e'd give someone a catch. We won by fifteen runs. Fifteen!"

Roy let the error pass—it sounded better than sixteen. "Good catch, Daphne," he said pointedly. He walked heavily over to her and picked up the ball. As he straightened, he met her eye. "That was a fantastic catch."

She blushed. "Sorry, Roy," she said softly.

Rose unfolded her arms and stretched. "I bet," she said with a yawn, "it din't arf 'urt yer 'and though, din't it Daphne?"

MANHUNT

August 1952

In the evening Mick returned from his mother's shopping trip, Pauline's baby-sitting duties were suspended and even Alan's ailments had eased. Will and Sam, the latter replete with a black eye, emerged with the younger children just as the shadows lengthened. "We're 'untin'," Derek told him as Roy arrived on the Green. "Two teams." He indicated the groups, each of about half-a-dozen children. "This is my team. We picked 'em afore you got 'ere. Oh yeah, 'n no goin' down the Ride nor in no gardens."

"What am I?" Roy asked.

"A stuck-up snob!" Derek enjoyed his joke, as did most of the others.

"I mean are we hunters or hunted?"

Daphne spoke from the midst of the second group, comprised mainly of the youngest ones. "We're bein' 'unted, Roy. I've told 'em some good places ter 'ide."

Hunting was a favourite. It gave excuse to roam the village, hunter or hunted. Roy enjoyed hunting, being vigilant and silent, tracking the quarry. But he preferred to be hunted, using his knowledge of the countryside, deploying stealth and cunning, bluffing pursuers. He felt in command, whether concealing himself in some hiding place, changing from one to another, or keeping on the move. He liked outwitting pursuers, laying false trails or striking for the signpost on the Green at an unexpected juncture or from an unanticipated direction. Touching the signpost without being intercepted was the main aim, while remaining undetected for the evening constituted a secondary victory. He could exploit what he knew of the others: those who were afraid of gloomy Spindle Wood, those who were lazy and would not search thoroughly, or the few who were systematic but slow.

Roy surveyed his group. Derek had been clever. Having made sure Roy's team had few resourceful members, he had removed the nearest obvious cover. Keeping out of private gardens was sensible with such numbers: there would soon be trouble if a grown-up discovered them trespassing. But the Ride led directly from behind the signpost to the Big House, where local landowners had lived, that was now a private school for girls. The old carriageway, pot-holed, was lined on both sides with trees and undergrowth. There were thick hedges on the outsides, cordoning off the avenue from the fields. It provided hiding-places very close to the finishing post. Putting it out of bounds made the task of Derek's team much simpler.

"I don't see why we can't use the Ride," protested Roy. "Some of these nippers will be caught before we've started. They can't run fast enough to get clear. They'll never reach Spindle Wood, or Roper's."

"We decided. I told yer. No goin' down the Ride."

"Well you make sure you count all the way to a hundred, then," Roy warned. "Don't skip any—and shut your eyes as well."

"I dun't cheat. You sayin' I cheat?" There was a profound silence. "Right then, starting—now! One, two, three…"

Roy stayed for the count to settle down, meanwhile encouraging his younger team-mates to disperse in at least two directions, though they were reluctant to separate. Sixteen—seventeen—eighteen… On twenty-two he told Rose to close her eyes and insisted the count be restarted.

"That's not the rules," Derek complained.

"The rules are that you count slowly and with your eyes shut. Rose was squinting, and she turned her face to follow me when I moved."

"You shun't be 'ere now, anyway," Rose chipped in.

"I'm staying put 'til I know you're not cheating."

"All right," conceded Derek. "Rose, keep yer eyes shut. One… two…"

Roy felt partly compensated for his defeat at cricket, and was doubly pleased as he silently withdrew, for he had gained valuable seconds for his team to scatter. Out of earshot, he loped down the lane. He intended to use the stile and turn sharp across three meadows to reach Spindle Wood. He had learnt never to start in the direction of his ultimate destination, because one of the hunters was bound to peep after him; moreover, he had deliberately named the wood as a red herring, for he would not remain there. Instead, he would keep moving, doubling back behind the hedges to approach the Green in the early part of the game. Nothing would please him more than to sit on the bench for the rest of the evening waiting for the hunters to return, with only the small fry captured.

Over the stile he was startled to come across Daphne, squatting low behind the hedge. "What are you doing here? I got extra time for you to skidaddle. You should be miles away by now!"

"I'm waitin' fer you. Yer goin' ter Spindle Wood, ain't yer?"

"How do you know?"

"Before you come, they was talkin'. Rose said you was a crafty bugger 'n yer'd go one way 'n double-back the other."

Roy felt a little less confident of his strategy.

"If they goes straight there they'll catch yer," Daphne continued. "Come wi' me instead. I got somewhere new."

So instead of crossing three fields, they traversed one, then turned to one side, keeping low along the hedge.

"You're going to the Ride. Out of bounds tonight. They said."

"Shh! We're only goin' alongside it. Come on." They hurried to the corner of the field, crawled through a hedge, then followed the line of trees and the overgrown bushes at the edge of the Ride. The next field was growing barley. Roy saw that the outside strip had been recently mown. At the end of the swathe a bulky green shape was visible. A few sheaves were scattered around, not yet collected into shocks. Daphne had not paused.

"Where're you going?"

"The binder. They dun't know it's 'ere."

The machine was covered by a large tarpaulin which hung limp in heavy folds down to the stubble. In places additional rolls billowed out across the shaven stalks. Daphne went quickly round to the far side, with Roy following. "'Elp us wi' this." She was panting from the crouching run she'd made down the field, and was now on her knees with her forearms reaching under the rumpled canvas.

Roy knelt, sliding his arms alongside hers. Together, they lifted. It was heavy, and as soon as there was headroom they began to squirm underneath. Roy felt the new stubble prick his legs as they wormed forward.

"Lift it 'igher," Daphne muttered. "I can't git under."

He felt the weight of the dense stuff on his back and shoulders, took a large gulp of air and, holding his breath, strained upwards. His arms slowly straightened.

"'S alright. I can get through now. C'm on."

Lowering his buttocks, Roy pulled himself along, drawing his feet out of sight as the tarpaulin resettled. "I can't see a thing," he whispered. The sun had warmed the tent to oven-pitch. Sweat ran into his eyes and down his body. "It's stifling."

"We better make a little tunnel where we come in,"

Daphne suggested. "We'll git some air then, an' we'll see 'em if they come." They tugged at the cover until a tunnel was formed. Then they noticed some sacks hanging over one of the cutting blades, and arranged them on the ground so that they could lie more comfortably. "Put yer feet tha' way," ordered Daphne, "then I c'n put me 'ead 'ere 'n look out." They rearranged themselves. As they did so, something scuttled in the blackness beyond them. "Rats, prob'ly," she observed.

"Cripes!"

"'S gone now. Scared stiff of us, I shun't wonder. I can see right up the field from 'ere," she continued, unperturbed. "We c'n close the tunnel if they come. They'll never know we're 'ere."

"If they come the way we did we won't see them."

"Yer'd prob'ly 'ear 'em though. Anyway, they wun't. They'll go ter Spindle Wood fust. Rose said. If they don't find us there they wun't come on 'ere 'cos they dun't know this is 'ere 'n the Ride's out 'o bounds ennit? So why should they?" This rigmarole made sense.

They lay still awhile. The heat lay over the field: the scent of newly-cut straw together with the stuffy atmosphere made Roy drowsy. "Daphne," he asked, "how did you know this was here?"

"Well there were one somewhere. C'nt yer 'ear it 's arternoon, when we was playing cricket?"

So that's what the throbbing had been, not heat-stroke after all...

"Let's change places," she suggested, "I'm gittin' cramp. Mind yer 'ead!" she warned, as Roy made to

111

stand. He ducked, partially lost balance and banged his leg on the towing arm of the binder.

"Ouch! That hurt!" he yelped. He could hear Daphne giggle while he rubbed his shin. "I bet it's bleeding." He was aware of her body gently vibrating. "Shh! It's not funny; it hurts."

"I said mind yer 'ead 'n yer did 'n then yer bashed yer leg instead." The words warbled over her laughter.

"It's grazed. Stop it! They'll hear you in Spindle Wood."

Daphne was writhing on the coarse canvas: the tent wall shook with her convulsions.

"Shut up! It bloody hurts!"

Daphne was stilled. He could feel her watching him.

"I ain't never 'eard you swear before, Roy, that I 'ain't."

Roy gingerly felt his leg. "I do, sometimes," he claimed, after a pause.

"'N yer goes ter church on Sundays and sings in the choir 'n all."

He wasn't sure if he was being teased or not. "'Course I swear when I want to." Perhaps he should swear more often, he thought.

He felt a hand brush his arm. "G'is yer leg. I'll suck it better."

"'S all right. It's not bleeding much, look. It's the bang that hurts." He moved his leg into the shaft of subdued sunlight. The rawness glowed purple, the graze surmounting a ripening bruise.

Daphne put her arms and head across his thigh, turning her face to the tunnel. "No one comin'," she concluded. "They'll be goin''ome, I shun't wonder, afore much longer."

"Bet they're sitting on the Green. They won't even have been looking for us. Cheats. Sitting there, nattering away, just pretending they've been looking. They're not hunters. They're scared in the woods when it's getting dark."

"Even Derek? Is he scared, d'yer think? Shall I tell 'im 'e's scared?"

"No, not Derek." He had to be fair. "But the rest of them."

"The rest of 'em dun't matter though, do they? I mean, really there's jist you 'n Derek, ain't there? Like this arternoon. It was jist you 'n 'im, weren't it?"

Roy had never openly acknowledged a serious rivalry. He wasn't convinced there was one. Derek was still his friend, wasn't he? "No one else could play though, could they? I mean, you and Rose can run and throw and catch. If you'd been on my side we'd have won."

"Am I better 'n Rose then?"

"Yeah! A lot! You're quicker, and you've got a good throw. You don't fall asleep like she does: you try!"

She moved her head below his knee. Her lips touched his sore shin. It was soft, soothing. "Yer've skinned it alright. Goodness!" Her tongue stung the graze, then her lips closed over it and the sharpness subsided.

They stayed like that as the light in the tunnel deepened. The call of an owl floated over from the Ride.

Daphne shivered, then sighed. "There's a real 'unter," she whispered.

Roy was leaning on one of the blades, taking his weight on one elbow, watching the silhouette of the top of her head against the blood-red glow behind her. "You still haven't said how you knew this was here."

"Dad come 'ome at tea-time 'n told us. Mr. Robertson'll test some o' what they cut tonight, an' if it's dry 'nuff they'll be cuttin' all o' this tomorrer. They bin cuttin' up at Jenkinson's, 'n all. ''S ready,' Dad reckons. 'E said 'You mark my words, 'arvest'll start tomorrer, whatever them tests says.'"

"How's he know for definite?"

Daphne slowly sat up. He could just make out her smile as she spoke. "'Cos Jacob's 'ere, 'e says. In the woodman's 'ut in Cottage Spinney. Dad saw some smoke so 'e went ter see. Jacob were skinning a rabbit what 'e'd caught."

The calling boys, the men with guns or sticks at the ready, the bolting hares, panicking pheasants, the jugs of lemonade keeping cool in the hedgerow, the bent women standing the shocks in wigwams; and later the smell of leather on the old shires pulling piled hay-carts home under the moon, and finally the hum of the thresher shaking away the last shreds of summer.

Roy peered at one of the blades above. Already there were strands of straw hanging down in wisps like torn cobwebs. "This was a good place to think of, Daphne," he said. He shifted position. "The sun's nearly gone."

The game ended at sunset, though the smaller children would have gone home earlier. Roy had settled for the minor victory of remaining undiscovered. He wondered what Derek's excuse would be for not finding him.

His reverie was interrupted. "D'yer want ter git back to the Green without any of 'em seein' us? Beat 'em all ends up?"

From her voice he could tell that she was eager, that she would relish such a triumph as much as he. But surely, they had left their move too late? "They'll be back there by now. We wouldn't have a chance."

Daphne persisted. "If we go back up the Ride we can creep up to them bushes 'n run out 'n touch the signpost afore they even know we's there."

"Can't use the Ride, can we? You put it out of bounds before I got there, didn't you?"

"Derek said that. It weren't me. It weren't no one else, only Derek."

"But we agreed."

"You 'eard what 'e said, though, din't yer? 'E said not ter go down the Ride, din't 'e?"

"Well there you are then." He could see no point in discussing it further.

"Roy, listen! We'd be comin', not goin', wun't we? Comin' back up it, see."

He looked towards her barely visible face in astonishment. "Crikey. That's brilliant!"

"Well? Shall us?"

"I don't know. It's sort of cheating." He paused. "Aren't you clever, though?" He had admired only her Auntie Jean outside his immediate family, except for

Churchill and Dennis Compton. He put his hand on her forearm. "Brilliant!"

"Come on then," she urged. She twisted towards the tunnel, and started to crawl down it. "Lift it up a bit," she called.

"Wait a minute," he replied. He wasn't sure.

"Wha's up?" Daphne's voice was muffled as she inched her way into the folds.

Everyone cheated. Derek cheated by picking the strongest team available. He'd say he wasn't out even if his stumps were flattened. He copied from Roy's exercise books or looked up the answer before he started a sum. Rose cheated. She'd say she wasn't playing tig any more then, when she was being ignored, would spring up to claim a victim. At rounders she would complain about the bowling so that she could receive more balls until she hit one of them. And she always jumped the queue at dinner-time, saying a place had been kept for her. Perhaps he and Daphne had been cheating this evening, as they weren't hiding in the vegetation or other customary place such as an old haystack or barn. But then, the binder was standing in a field, just as evident as the corn amidst which they could have concealed themselves—corn that wouldn't be there tomorrow.

Roy felt his pulse bumping in his chest. There would be a moment when he could decide. He could feel Daphne watching him from inside the tunnel. His calf muscles tensed, ready to thrust him forward. A shiver ran down his spine. "Yes!" The word hissed, lingering between them.

"C'mon, then. 'Ave to 'urry up!"

They slithered out, sniffing the dampening air. Roy's back was stiff, and his leg smarted when he stretched his weight on it. He stumbled after Daphne over the field. She found a gap in the hedge and they hurried along the old carriageway for the centre of the village. Roy's movement became easier with the exercise.

"It'll be dark in a coupla minutes," Daphne said. "Race yer back'ards ter the yews!"

They staggered backwards in the gloom, their gait unsteady as they floundered along. Their arms flailed, striving for speed. Roy's knuckles caught Daphne's elbow, making her stagger. She clutched his arm to keep upright, pulling him off-balance. They collapsed to the crumbling tarmac, out of breath and giggling. She scrambled to her feet. "Dead 'eat," she laughed.

"You're brilliant," he said again.

"Bet I dun't pass me eleven-plus next year like you 'ave, though. I wish I were really clever."

"You are, Daphne. Thinking of this, for a start."

"Any fool c'n be cleverer than Derek."

"Well I didn't think of it, did I?"

They had passed the yew trees, and could make out the gateway and lighter sky beyond the Ride. The last rays of sun touched the top branches of the plane tree that stood behind the Ploughman's Rest. "At least he can't say it's after sunset," Roy said. With the dark mass of the yews behind them, they could risk walking along the centre of the Ride until the last few yards, when they moved to the side, dropped to all fours and crawled up to the bushes that flanked the gateway itself.

Derek and Rose were on the bench with their backs to them. Roy could hear their voices. He saw Derek turn to peer into the shadows down the lane which Roy had first taken, while Rose continued to murmur. Daphne crept alongside Roy behind the last, straggly rhododendron. "Can you 'ear 'em?" she whispered.

"Said they'd be nattering," Roy smirked.

"But can you 'ear what they're on about?" she persisted.

"No. Why?"

"Huh!" There was a pause before she slowly smiled. "Dun't matter," was all she said.

Roy nudged her gently with his elbow. "One," he prompted.

"Two," she whispered in reply.

"Three!" they bellowed together, bursting through the thin screen of leaves and lunging across the grass to hug the signpost.

Derek and Rose shot up from the bench and swung round.

"Beat yer! Beat yer twice over," shouted Daphne. "Beat yer 'cos yer din't find us 'n beat yer again 'cos we made it 'ome 'n yer never saw us comin'!"

Derek opened his mouth, no doubt to protest, but Daphne didn't give him a chance. "Beat yer, beat yer!" she sang, whirling round the signpost as if it were a maypole. Derek turned to Roy, arms outstretched in appeal; but Roy had collapsed onto the grass, arms pressed to his stomach to contain his laughter. He didn't want to antagonise Derek further. He could have made no coherent answer had Derek formed a question. Daphne's feet flew around the signpost, more off the ground than on it. Her gyrations synchronised with her chant, "Beat yer! Beat yer! No-ball! No-ball!"

"I'm a-goin'," Rose chimed. Derek was so enraged he didn't seem to hear her. Rose took a pace towards him, shouting in his ear. "I shall 'ave ter go in now, or me mum'll belt me one."

Derek remained with his arms aloft before Roy, but his face was turned to Daphne, eyes following her movement as if mesmerised. "Are you comin', or are yer gonna stand there like a scarecrow?" Rose grabbed one of his arms and tugged, making him move his feet. He stepped a few awkward paces back, then pulled free.

Daphne at last paused, leaning against the signpost, panting for breath, exultant. Derek turned his attention to Roy, who had crawled to the bench, on which he was now leaning, still trying not to laugh. "You two cheated. We caught all the rest, easy. 'N you two dun't count 'cos yer cheated."

Rose had been fidgeting with impatience. Now she joined Derek, who had been stranded in no man's land between Daphne and Roy, between being a hunter and going home for supper. "It's mothers 'n fathers tomorrer, remember," she announced. "They can't cheat at that. Come on Derek."

Roy laughed at last, watching them merge into the quickening shadows. He hauled himself onto the bench, where he lay on his back with his legs drawn up. He became aware of the graze tingling in the cooler air as Daphne flopped down in front of the bench. "She's mad with you, Daphne," he said. "She didn't even wait for you to walk home."

Daphne snorted. "Mothers and fathers my foot! She wun't 'arf git a surprise tomorrer. You know why she wants ter play that? She sez they'm pretendin' ter be married, at least 'til we go ter school agin. Well," she added, "their school."

Roy was puzzled. "Who?"

"'Er'n Derek o' course."

"What for?"

"'Cos o' the other day. In Spindle Wood."

"What?"

"She sez they were up there collectin' wood."

"Already? That's early."

"'S what she says. 'N she took 'er knickers down 'n showed 'im."

"Showed him what?"

Daphne looked up at him. "What yer think? Cor, yer a bit slow on the uptake, ain't yer?"

Roy was dumbfounded. Daphne sighed. "She took 'er knickers down 'n lifted up 'er dress 'n showed 'im. An' then," she went on, deliberately, "'e took 'is trousers 'n pants down 'n showed 'er. So now she's always in 'is team 'n when we play mothers 'n fathers they'll be married, like."

The blue of the day had now turned to indigo. The moon had risen, and the trees of the Ride became a dark mass. Daphne sat up, legs spread-eagled on the damp grass. "We could get married, too, if yer like. Pretend married. If yer want."

"Us? What, now?" Roy could feel his face prickling. "You and me?" He sensed her eyes searching him. "Like them, you mean?"

"Yeah. Now. Down the Ride." She scratched her leg where the stubble had scrubbed. "What d'yer reckon?" She rubbed again, leaving the skirt of her dress above her knee.

"I don't know... I never..." He tailed off.

She bent her leg so she could reach her calf more easily. "I'm gonna itch all over ternight." There was a dim splash of white beyond the hem of her dress. "I've got chaff in me knickers already," she chuckled, "'n 'arvest ain't 'ardly started yit."

From the way her head tilted, Roy knew she was still watching him, though he could not see her expression. Then there was stillness between them, taught and tangible, stretching to the first bright star shimmering in the August night.

"One day, soon, then, p'raps." She stood. "Time ter go."

She reached towards him, offering her hands. He took them, and levered himself up, then she leant back and pulled him towards her. They each took the other's weight and balanced there a moment. Then she leant forward on tiptoe and kissed him on the lips. Salt, sweat, blood. "I like the taste o' you," she murmured.

He could smell her hair in his face. He had fallen with her, hadn't he, down the Ride? Rose's sister had fallen, Rose had said. But did falling over backwards count? And then he saw words that he had never used flashed up across the sky, and heard words that he wasn't saying tumbling over each other inside him.

"It's a nice taste," she said. "An' as fer gettin' married, well, it'd be too dark ter see now, wun't it?" With that, she let go, spun away from him and skipped off down the road. "Beat yer! Snowball, beat yer! Snowball."

He chased after her, joining in her canter and her wild chant, joining in her hilarity, her energy, her rhythm, as they sprang and twirled and zig-zagged along the road until they reached her garden gate which she opened, closed and leant against all in one action.

"It were me what showed yer the binder, Roy, weren't it? It'll be 'arvest tomorrer, right ter the end o' the 'olidays. An' them two fatheads dun't even know it. 'Night Roy."

He watched her shape blend into the darkness of the house. "Goo'night," he called softly, waiting until he heard the door close behind her.

The moon had climbed above the plane tree, throwing a silver sheen on the road and the garden fences as he passed other cottages in Daphne's row. He reached the playing-field and, on impulse, veered through the gateway and headed for the swings. He should have been home ages ago, but it was so intoxicating to thrust through the moonlight and pull at the chains, to lean back and watch the emergent stars rush across the sky, to and fro, to and fro. The squeak of the chains synchronised with the surges of energy pouring through him, and the moon swept into vision and out again as the world turned about him; deep inside him and far, far away, he heard again the throb of the binder and the pulse of Daphne's laughter. From the blackness under the elms he imagined her whisper, ''S only a game, Roy.' He allowed the swing to slow until, finally, it rested.

Remember this moment, he thought. Just don't forget, that's all. Then he flung himself forward, clear of the trodden earth below the swing, and fell onto the grass, where his sobs were muffled and his tears mingled with the thickening dew.

THE TOWER FUND

December 1954

Each Sunday morning Roy checked the hand-drawn thermometer pasted on the notice-board next to the bell ropes. At best its lifeblood inched up, pound by pound, though thousands were needed. Sometimes weeks would pass with no movement. At this rate the church tower would never be repaired. How could he help?

He'd sung in the choir for at least eight years, enduring the amused stares of girls from the private school sat in the stalls opposite. There were twenty, though he hardly heard them even in the most uplifting hymns, for they were obliterated by the rustic roar of Stan the roadman's baritone—always in unison but consistently a quarter-tone sharp—or distorted by Mr. Ford's tremulous tenor: both men sat behind him. To one side would be Daphne and Derek, when they attended, and Beryl, daughter of the church organist, with a friend from the Women's Institute. From his left came the enfeebled voices of the congregation, ever more wavering as time went on.

There had been occasional relief from this

cacophony when it had been his turn to pump air into the organ. He sat on the stool next to Beryl's mother, incurring an occasional rap on the knuckles from her should he allow the block of wood on its string to fall below the pencilled line. But at least he was removed from the choir and his back was turned on those embarrassing schoolgirls. Since electricity now powered the organ, these occasions no longer occurred.

However, since he had gone to the grammar school, singing had become a pleasure. An enterprising church choir rendered High Anglican settings of introits, services, canticles and anthems. He relished the works of England's finest composers of church music, Byrd, Purcell, Parry and Darke among them. Now, as autumn deepened, he had the idea of organising carol-singing: that is what he would do for the Tower Fund. What better than carols at a time of goodwill, visiting every nook of the scattered parish? His brother had done the same years before. That was his inspiration.

On that previous occasion he had been one of a dozen or so singers to have given and received genuine joy. He recalled warming himself before the Squire's log fire, a small glass of punch in hand, the camaraderie in the Ploughman's where customers joined in a rousing Hark, the Herald Angels Sing! On the final evening lanes were so illumined by stars they didn't need their hurricane lamps: the fields shone, making Christmas a special time. Bolstered by these memories he set about organising the event.

Reverend Fox wouldn't allow carol sheets to be taken

out of the cupboard in the vestry for fear of them being damaged. Beryl offered to make copies.

"There's six of us from the choir, and four more have promised to come," Roy told her.

He had to let his intention be known to PC Anderson, who was at first suspicious, but when Roy mentioned Beryl and Mr. Ford, and added that some younger adults would also take part, he demurred.

"You let me know the dates, and what parts of the village you'll visit on any given night, and I'll—as long as you stick to it, mind—I'll give my consent," was his enthusiastic response.

Thus, at seven o'clock on a cool Wednesday evening, a group of eight met on the village green to embark on this charitable progress. Roy was pleasantly surprised to see Rose, as she never went to church. He supposed she wanted to be with Derek—perhaps they were still pretending to be married... He suggested they wait a few minutes for the others.

"No point," Derek said. "Bet they wun't turn up."

"I've got the carol sheets here, Roy. Mother copied them for me. Only the words, but we know the tunes anyway." Beryl distributed them, and they agreed an order for the first few houses. There were no latecomers, but four adults would ensure discipline and motivation were maintained—reassuring, with Derek and Rose present.

"We're doing the whole village," Roy told them, "including Church Cottages, Wood End, Warren Hill and Fourways."

"What, all in one night?" Rose queried.

"'Course not. Two nights for the village and two for the rest."

Derek stopped in his tracks. "Four? Yer din't say we was doin' four nights. I en't doin' that many."

"Shall we make a start?" proposed Mr. Ford in a voice as tentative as when he sang.

The first evening went well. Despite occasional discords, the carols were sung with vigour, except by the young adults, Valerie and Ronald, who proved timid singers. Roy placed himself near them, staying in unison to help them.

"Dun't keep standin' be'ind them two," Daphne whispered as they passed the field before the next houses.

"Why not?"

"Them'll think yer watchin' 'em. They en't come 'ere fer the singin'."

"Why are they here, then?"

"Gormless, you are. They're gittin' married next year. Tha's why they've bin to church, see? They'm a-courtin'."

The cottages here were terraced, so one carol served several homes. By half-past nine one main street had been covered. Roy suggested continuing to the Ploughman's, making inroads into the next evening, but he was thwarted by Rose. "Can't go down there," she pointed. "It's me cousin's. We'll wake the baby. Anyway, can't sing no more. Me voice is goin'. Yer bin singin' too 'igh fer me, specially that Way in a Manger."

Beryl intervened. "You should have said something, dear. I'll bring Mother's tuning fork tomorrow, then we can choose the correct key."

"I have some lozenges," said Mr. Ford, "if they'll help."

Rose ignored him. "Can't come tomorrer. Got ter wash me sister's 'air. She can't bend over the sink no more."

The next evening was colder, an easterly wind driving sleet before it.

"Me pages is all soggy from last night," Derek grumbled, "'n I can't 'old 'em still ter read 'em. Can I 'ave another lot what I can read?"

"I'm sorry," Beryl replied, "but I don't seem to have any spares. I must have mislaid them. Just as well we know them all by heart."

"Well I dun't, see? So it's a waste o' time me bein' 'ere, ennit?"

Roy confronted him "Well, which ones do you know?"

"I en't clever, like you—"

Daphne interrupted. "I bet you know summat. I bet you know the first verse of While Shepherds Watched. All on us knows that."

So for the next stops they sang just that, though on one occasion Roy jabbed Derek in the ribs to stop his rendition, which concerned the washing of socks. When there was no response at one house, they sang the verse again.

"Borin'," Derek muttered.

"Your fault. Anyway, if you used your torch and

128

stood with your back to the rain you could read the rest of it."

"Batteries'r goin'."

Roy felt he could batter Derek, but said nothing.

They moved down the road, coming to four detached houses, the only new homes in the village since the war. There was no answer from the first, where a light beamed in the porch. A bluish glow flickered behind the curtains of the second, but again no one came to the door.

"They'm be watchin' their television set," concluded Daphne. "Prob'ly can't 'ear us."

"Well," said Derek, "I fer one can't sing any louder. En't goin' ter bust meself tryin'."

Roy sighed. Beryl suggested they move on. The front door of the third house opened as they approached.

"Happy Christmas!" Beryl began.

"Who are you?"

"We're carol-singing to raise funds for the church tower."

"Oh yeah? We've just had a bunch of kids claiming the same thing. Anyway, we're Chapel, so you needn't waste your time. Goodnight." The door was banged shut.

"Well!" Beryl turned to the others. The weak pinpoint of light from Derek's torch revealed her shocked expression.

"Stuck-up so-and-so," added Daphne. "Let's miss the next one out 'n git ter the pub."

"I'll have to leave you at this stage. I may rejoin you

later." Mr. Ford pointed his umbrella into the wind and strode off.

Beryl said, "I'm popping across the road to see that Mother's comfortable. She'll have gone to bed by now. Come across when you've been to the Ploughman's and have a warm. I'll put some milk on for a cup of Ovaltine."

"Why's old Ford gone?" Derek asked.

"I think he's tee-total," ventured Valerie.

"Glad I'm not," said her fiancé. "We'll nip in and warn them. Have a whip round."

Under the lamp in the porch of the Ploughman's Rest, the trio chose a different carol, Lullay, Lullay, My Little Tiny Child. This was their best singing thus far, the unaffected treble voices suiting the lilting melody. Encouraged, Roy improvised an alto line, and there followed a few bars in the second verse when he felt a shiver run down his spine that had nothing to do with the bitter wind. During the third verse Derek turned on him. "Yer puttin' me orf. Jist sing the tune. Swankin' agin."

They restarted, but were overwhelmed by a rising, raucous chorus of God Rest You Merry Gentlemen emanating from inside. They stopped singing and stared at each other.

"Bloody hell!" said Roy.

Daphne stepped up to the door and pushed it open. The voices swelled, wafted by the smell of stale ale. She went inside.

"Where's them two cissies gone? Forgotten all about us, 'avin' a nice drink, I bet." Before Roy could reply

Daphne was thrust outside. A man's voice followed. "You ain't old enuff to come in 'ere. Sling yer 'ook. Bloody kids! Bugger orf. I'm fed up wi' tellin' yer."

Daphne half-stumbled down the steps. "Bully!" she called over her shoulder as the door closed.

"What's he saying? Didn't you tell him what we're doing?"

"Din't git a chance. Said 'e'd 'ad another lot round 'ere tonight an' if we din't clear off e'd call the police."

"That's the second time someone's said that. It's not fair. We were the ones who got permission. Who else is there?"

"Don't ask me," said Derek.

Inside Beryl's house they huddled round an oil-heater, clutching mugs of warm milk. Beryl said she'd speak to the landlord in the morning and notify PC Anderson about an apparently illegal group.

"'Ooever it is is in front'v us," Daphne observed, "so no wonder folks are fed up."

"We en't goin' ter take much then," sniffed Derek. "What we git last night?"

"Just over five pounds."

"'Zat all?"

"It's not too bad. Last night was down the poorer bit."

"It's the spirit that counts," said Beryl.

The weather worsened, their voices weakened. Neither Mr. Ford nor Valerie and Donald rejoined them, and although they were welcomed in a handful of homes it was hard to remain enthusiastic. As they parted Derek announced that he wouldn't be coming again. His torch batteries were flat and he could feel a cold coming on, so he wouldn't be able to sing in any case.

"At least I bet there won't be another group carolling where we're going tomorrow," Roy said.

Beryl asked "Do you want to carry on, Roy? You don't have to, you know."

"I do. I do have to. I promised. I promised the vicar, I promised the Squire and I promised PC Anderson. And I promised all—both—of you. And myself." He felt to be near to tears to think he might fail, and of the excuses he would have to make in self-justification.

"'Course yer did," said Daphne.

On the third night, there was, predictably, no Valerie or Donald, no Rose or Derek. But Mr. Ford was there, and between them, with Daphne holding the tune, Beryl supplying contralto and Roy offering a bass line, albeit an octave higher, they at last made a sound pleasant enough to warrant reward. They were further cheered by a donation of one pound ten shillings from the landlord of the Ploughman's by way of apology for the previous evening's misunderstanding. There was much tramping to be done to outlying hamlets and farms, often down muddy tracks, and there were several untethered dogs to negotiate. But at least the barking brought people to their doors, and twice they were invited in for sherry, with a glass of orange juice for Mr. Ford; thus, when the quartet regained the village green at the end of their route they were in buoyant spirits.

"Well done, Daphne, and you Roy. And thank you very much, Mr. Ford, for turning out again. Goodnight everybody. See you tomorrow."

The adults went their separate ways. Roy took Daphne's arm. He felt her surprise. "I know where all the puddles are," he explained, steering her down the road. "I didn't expect to see Mr. Ford again."

"Bet she asked him, 'speshly."

"You think so?"

"Yeah. And wun't be surprised if she din't put that thirty bob in 'erself. She wants this to work, Roy."

"Well, she supports everything to do with the church—flowers, graves, the choir, reading lessons and everything."

"'S more 'n that, Roy. She wants it to work fer you." She stopped walking so Roy let go of her arm. "And so do I."

"It's for the Tower Fund, Daphne, not for me."

"Daft, y'are." She suddenly stepped to him and gave him a kiss. Before he could think of whether to respond—and in what manner—she'd moved away. "C'mon, it's gittin' windy," she called, as if nothing had happened.

Overnight that same wind brought snow, about a foot of it. By evening most people had cleared their front paths, and Stan had uncovered the footpath at the side of the road. Roy, nursing a sore throat that developed into a cold with bouts of shivering, headed for the Green again, not knowing what or who to expect. The other three stalwarts were already there. Beryl had brought an extra lamp and Mr. Ford carried a shovel. "Just in case. This wind's coming all the way from the Steppes with nothing to stop it."

Beyond the centre of the village roads were just passable. Where they could they trod in the ruts left by a recent cart; elsewhere they ploughed through snow that reached the top of their Wellingtons. It was a mile and a half to the church and its cluster of cottages. Roy felt the burden of the bag of coins he intended to give to the vicar.

At first, he found singing difficult, but gradually his throat loosened, and he began to feel better. "Right," he said. "About half-a-mile to Bowman's farm, then on to Wood End."

"What about the Vicarage, Roy?"

"Leaving it 'til last. We've got to come back this way anyway."

The shovel was useful in a couple of places where there were gaps in the hedge, but they continued resolutely and by ten o'clock were heading back, first calling on Stan's home, nestling in the row of thatched cottages opposite the church. Stan was sitting by a blazing fire, wrapped in an army blanket. "I'd o' come wiv yer," he said, "but I were out in it all day. I were all mornin' clearing the footpath to the village. 'Ad a pint in the Ploughman's, and be the time I come out the wind 'd blowed it all back agin."

"Well I'll be blowed," muttered Daphne, making Roy giggle.

Beryl suggested they sing Silent Night but Stan succumbed to a bout of coughing, so they gave up after one verse, wished him a Merry Christmas and crossed the road, passing through the lych gate into the churchyard.

"Gives me the creeps," said Daphne.

"Look, the light's on in the hall," said Roy.

"The last port of call," observed Mr. Ford.

Beryl laughed. "With due respect, Mr. Ford, a glass of port would suit me very nicely."

As they brushed snow from the overhanging rhododendrons and forced open the wicket gate to the vicarage, the light went out.

"Couldn't have heard us coming," Roy said.

"The snow will have deadened everything," said Mr. Ford.

"We'll have to sing loudly, then," remarked Beryl. "Let's choose a jolly one. Roy?"

"Daphne, you choose."

"God Rest You Merry Gentlemen. We ain't done that since the Ploughman's"

"After four," directed Beryl. "Nice and fast now, one-and-two-and-three-and-four…"

They sang with as much gusto as they could muster. 'Tidings of comfort and joy' rang out for the last time. Followed by silence. No light appeared. Daphne hammered on the door as Beryl tugged the bell-rope, to no avail. "Well, what do you suggest we do, Mr. Ford?"

"He must be in the kitchen, round the back. I'll have a look. Pass me the shovel, Roy, if you please."

The others waited, stamping their feet in the porch. After a few moments they heard the scrunch of boots as Mr. Ford came round the corner of the house. "No sign of him anywhere, I'm afraid."

"But the light was on. I saw it."

"Yes Roy."

"Then it went off."

They returned to the village, heads down, shoulders hunched against the wind sweeping in from the Fens. Silent night, holy night.

Before Daphne trudged down her garden path, she scraped the gate into place and leant over it. "I want ter whisper summat," she said. She pulled him to her and kissed him. Her skin was like ice, and her eyes shone like stars, but somehow her lips were warm and her tongue, when she pushed it into his mouth, was burning. "Don't catch my cold," he said. "I reckon it'll be 'flu."

"Bugger yer cold." She kissed him again.

This time he responded, feeling that same surge he'd experienced, two years ago, when his elation had spurred him to soar to the skies. Daphne wrenched away from him and floundered through the snow to her front door.

Roy duly went down with 'flu, missing all the Christmas services. He counted the carol-singing proceeds several times in the days that followed, returning to the church for Low Sunday matins, celebrated by a sparse congregation and a choir of three.

He removed his cassock in the vestry and placed the coin bag on the side table. "It's from the carol singing, Reverend, for the Tower Fund." He sneezed.

"Ah," said Reverend Fox.

"Sixteen pounds, twelve shillings and fourpence-ha'penny."

"I see."

Roy watched while the vicar emptied the bag, trapping the two banknotes under a candlestick and sorting the coins into piles. Roy sneezed again.

Reverend Fox completed his addition. "Tuppence short, I believe." He raised an eyebrow. Roy took the bag he'd borrowed from his grandad's shop and felt inside. He found some coins trapped in a corner fold and handed them over. "Another penny, a ha'penny and two farthings."

"Ah," said the Reverend.

Daphne had waited under the lych gate to walk with Roy back to the village. The road was covered in slush, impacted where a few cars had passed. "These boots are slippy," she said, taking his arm to keep her balance.

"Didn't even say thank you," Roy complained. "And I bet he heard us the other night. What sort of vicar is he? Wish we'd taken some of it for ourselves."

"Like Rose, you mean?"

"Like what?"

"Rosie. Derek told me. I reckon 'e knew about it all along."

"What?" he repeated.

"Rose. The second night, Thursday. She 'n Mick 'n a

coupla others went carol singin' on their own. They did the posh houses in Barn Lane and the Ploughman's afore we did. Must've gone ter the back o' the pub so's Beryl's mum wun't 'ear 'em. Then they went 'ome in case we caught up wiv 'em."

"I don't believe it."

"'S true."

"How do you know?"

"I saw Mick 'n told 'im off fer not comin' wiv us when 'e said 'e would, 'n 'e said 'e 'ad bin singin' see, so there. S'pose it jist slipped out. Then 'e said don't tell anyone 'cos Derek would 'it 'im."

"Derek?"

"Yis, Roy, Derek. 'E organised it 'n Rose did it. She bullied Mick into it, 'n Will 'n Sam 'n all. Then she gave 'em 'alf a crown each to keep quiet. They reckon she got near on ten quid."

"The dirty, sly, blasted, filthy bugger! I'll bloody kill him! No wonder he wasn't at church this morning."

"'E wun't be comin' agin, bet yer. 'Is dad made 'im go ter git 'im out 'o the 'ouse while 'e 'ad a lie-in, but 'e's not on shifts no more so it dun't matter now."

Roy kicked a lump of half-frozen slush, slipped, and would have fallen but for grabbing Daphne to keep upright.

"Derek 'n Rose, Roy. People like them always win. They'll cheat if they 'ave to. Dun't say nothin' to 'em. T'ain't worth it."

"Next time I see him I'll—"

"No yer wun't, Roy. Yer wun't a-known nothin' 'bout it if I 'an't said, would yer? Yer'll only make trouble. I 'as ter go ter school wiv 'em, remember. 'N I promised Mick I wun't say anythin' 'cos 'e were scared stiff."

"Mick always was scared stiff."

"Dun't you 'ave bullies at your school? No, I dun't s'pose yer do. Not like Derek, any'ow. P'raps I shun't o' said nothin', but yer were so disappointed we din't take that much I thought it were only fair to tell yer. I might as well tell yer summat else, 'n all. I shan't be comin' to church no more, neither. I got a job at the Ploughman's, Sunday mornins, clearin' up fer a coupla hours from Sat'day nights. I start next weekend. New Year."

"Job? You're not old enough."

"'E dun't care. No one'll see me. I'll be finished afore openin' time. 'S only the same as you 'elpin' out in yer grandad's shop."

"It's not. He doesn't pay me anything."

"More fool you, then."

Roy felt he was slipping now, though he and Daphne were still walking with linked arms. Daphne? Not in the choir? "There'll be hardly anyone left."

"There's all them posh schoolgirls opposite, when they're not on 'oliday," she teased.

"I don't count them."

"I does. I've stared 'em all out, one by one. I start one end, wiv the one 'oo puts 'er glasses on ter sing, and goes all along the row. There's one tries ter stare me out, but she always blinks afore I do."

"I don't even look at them."

"Anyway, Roy, I ain't religious."

"But you go every week. And you've just done all this carol-singing."

"Maybe, but I ain't religious. I might as well tell yer the truth. I got two reasons. First, Sundays en't much fun in our 'ouse. Dad gits drunk most Sat'day nights, 'n 'e 'as a temper on 'im next day, I can tell yer. So I might as well be in the pub, out the way."

They slithered up hill, coming to the Green. "We've had a lot of fun round here, haven't we Daphne?" He could sense tears welling. He bunched a ball of slush and hurled it at the sign bearing the village name, the Coronation memento all villages had at their centre. Despite his sodden gloves, the action helped him regain some self-control. "I don't believe in God, either. Not anymore. Not with the Vicar, and now this, this Derek thing."

After Daphne had tramped through the ashes spread along her garden path, Roy finished his journey through the slush, swallowing hard to ease his throat, stemming tears. He'd not be friends with Derek or Rose again. He'd forget all about keeping in with Mick just so he could watch the Cup Final on his dad's television set, and he wouldn't believe anything that went on in church, except the music. As he turned through his own garden gate, he knew he hadn't told Daphne what was upsetting him, nor had he thought to ask her what had been her second reason.

GDAE

October 1955

I had my reasons for not entering that field. Some were logical. When you think about it, why would I want to reach over the stile, often muddy from someone's shoes, carefully place my violin case on the far side, toss my satchel after, then throw my rugby boots over, only to have to pick them all up again fifteen seconds later? And do it all again over the second stile on the far side of the field? Yes, this was the official route of the public footpath, which is why the stiles were there, but instead, before the first one I could walk seven paces to the right, turn left and continue down the parallel cartway on the other side of the hedge. Forty seconds and mud on my uniform to climb over the stiles, set against ten seconds to make the dogleg, cancelled out by another ten seconds saved at the other end, equivalent to another seven paces, because I was on the right of the path and needed to turn in that direction to continue to the bus stop. Moreover, I avoided the nuisance of having to juggle my luggage twice over. Like those problems we had in Maths: If a boy weighing seven-stone-six takes forty seconds to climb over two stiles whilst transporting rugby boots, violin case and satchel weighing eleven and a half pounds, how much energy. .

Then there was the business of tuning the violin. There was no time to do that after Geography. The rush along the crowded corridor and up the precipitous spiral staircase to the music room allowed no delay. Lateness meant Detention, so before leaving home I would tune up, exasperated by the ill-fitting peg of the A string and the fine adjustment needed for the E. Arriving out of tune merited Lines: I must ensure that I and my instrument are ready... But the thing was invariably discordant anyway after being carried along with rugby boots, which, with their long laces draped round my neck, reached the same height above the ground as my violin case. Walking had to be smooth, otherwise the regular collision with the boot—usually the left one, but not always—would make the violin rock in its case. Any turbulence sent it out of tune. I would hear the soft thrum of the sound box on each placement of my left foot, my ear cocked for the slightest shift in the haunting arpeggio of the open strings.

Admittedly, the cartway itself was frequently muddy. But if I skirted the worst puddles so that soil would collect only on the soles of my shoes, during the day it would dry, harden and drop off on pavements, in corridors and various classrooms. Whereas if I crossed the field the uppers could be saturated, leaving me wet-footed. That wouldn't have been so bad on Thursdays, because Maths came first. I sat by the wall, next to a heating pipe, and from November half-term until

Easter I could slip my shoes off and... If it takes a boy forty minutes to dry his feet on a six-inch circumference heating pipe emitting fifty-two and a half degrees Fahrenheit, how damp were his socks...? But there were days other than Thursday, when I might sit with wet feet until mid-afternoon. It's true I didn't carry violin and boots every day, but often enough to make the cartway the better choice.

The real reason, however, was that I had no wish to follow in my father's footsteps. He was a cussed man, and took the awkward route across the field on his way to work. The cartway was on private land, and he would stick to the rules. One dark January morning he'd hurried through a thick ground mist, hauled his bike over the first stile and stumbled into a sleeping cow. Bugger the blasted... The beast lumbered to its feet and fled in one direction while my father picked himself up and cycled off in the other to make up the lost seconds in order to catch the bus. I'd heard this story years previously. It seemed alarming, though everyone else laughed. It was silly, I suppose, but I kept my distance from large animals, and even when the field contained only dried-up cow-pats I was disinclined to use it.

Here's another problem for you. Part One: A man cycles on a rough path for twenty minutes at seven miles per hour. Calculate how much energy he uses in doing so. Part Two: Estimate the additional energy consumed if, after ten minutes, he stumbles into an obstacle, falls over, gasps, curses, then continues at nine miles per hour to complete his journey. $E \times Y + ? = !$

Of course in all this is the assumption that the bus

would be on time. It usually was, though it could be held up by cows being driven out after milking. Or a new driver might continue over crossroads at the old windmill instead of turning left, necessitating a tortuous reverse while the conductor walked behind, or in front really, waving a borrowed school scarf to alert any oncoming traffic. And on one occasion all the passengers had to get off to push the bus through the snow up Warren Hill (plenty of soggy socks that day).

I caught the eight-twenty bus six mornings a week. I was often late returning home—there were choir, after-school games and several societies I'd been told to join. On Sundays I still sang in the village church, but often had school services in town later in the day. So, I rarely saw the other village children, and when I did, we didn't have much to talk about. Those in my year, like Derek, went to a school as different from mine as was the village school we'd left behind. Their yarns were about teachers and children, bullies and cissies all unknown to me. Even the subjects they took included things I'd never heard of. The spontaneous gatherings of village children, taken for granted only fifteen months previously, no longer happened—or if they did it was without me. What were their lives like now? I had no idea about their preoccupations, their fears and ambitions, or even their games, if they still played any.

I was thinking about this one evening on my way home along the cartway. I was slower than usual, encumbered by satchel, rugby boots and violin case, and I kept stopping to shuffle leaves in search of chestnuts. I wondered if the others still played conkers. Maybe I could find one large enough to challenge all-conquering Derek. I turned a promising chestnut over with my foot. I put everything down to pick it up. Whilst stooping I heard strange sounds coming from the field, through the hedge. It might have been a cow, snuffling as it extended its neck towards some out-of-reach delicacy, but as I listened, I realised the noises were human grunts and groans. I peered into the hedge, but there was still sufficient foliage to conceal whatever was beyond it. The noises increased, with thuds and thumps. Then it dawned on me: two men were fighting.

There was a cry of pain. Instinctively I knew it was made by the voice of a stranger, and somehow that made things worse. I froze. The hedge shook as something crashed into it, and someone thrashed about at its base. I must escape! If I were discovered, their combined fury might be turned on me. I couldn't help being there, and I couldn't help hearing them. But if they saw me, I would be guilty, simply of being a witness.

Under the noise of the struggle it wouldn't matter if I splashed in puddles or kicked up leaves, and it wouldn't matter now how badly the violin went out of tune. But as I rounded the corner close to the stile the sounds stopped. Silence. Ahead of me were the crunchy cinders of the path between two ploughed fields. Around me was a calm I dare not disturb. Behind me were unknown terrors.

Softly, I put everything down, dropping to all fours. Hidden by the hedge I inched to the opening made for the stile. From ground level I saw only grass, the distant thatched roofs of a row of cottages and the skeletal timbers of a house being built in the far corner of the field. I raised myself a little. The further stile came into view, along with the trodden path that led to it. I leant to my left with all my weight resting on one hand. Then I saw them.

Yards away, his legs in the brambles, one man bent over another, whom he gripped in a headlock. His free hand held aloft a broken fence-post coiled by rusty barbed wire. Above the undergrowth I could see the head of the second man, strands of grass and twigs caught in his sandy hair. As I watched, this scarecrow jerked his shoulders, trying to get free.

What could I do? I thought of P.C. Anderson, probably off-duty and asleep, not welcoming a knock on his door. My mother came to mind, busy with cooking or ironing, tired of preposterous stories and half-truths. I thought of myself, helpless, and of the poised fence-post.

Later, recalling that tableau, I wondered who were the men—and why fighting? Nightmares repeatedly suggested how it ended—was there any alternative to the post cracking down on the skull, the barbed wire ploughing into the scalp? Decades later I still wake to that image, unable to go back to sleep. Was the money repaid, the woman returned, the damage made good? Honour restored, integrity preserved? And does it matter a jot to anyone now living?

The cartway has long since become a service road: sleeping policemen and warnings of children at play. The field spawned a score of homes. Even the cottages have been transformed into a mews development. Few villagers will recall the meadow with its stiles, and none would find a description of any interest.

Yet I imagine in, say, the house on the corner plot, a young boy woken by a brilliant winter moon before dawn, a boy who might draw back the curtain to see, to his surprise, a thick ground-mist layering the tarmac pavement and the privet bordering the garden. I wonder whether that boy could, for an instant, mistake his father's car, snug under its tarpaulin, for a cow lying on the lawn just where someone might walk into it. Bugger the blasted animal!

And in the first autumnal gale, with chestnut leaves whipping along the gutter, might that same boy be disturbed by bumps and crashes as the garden gate slams and the lap fencing shudders? If so, he will wake to billowing curtains in the shriek of the wind. If he dares himself to get out of bed, he'll close the window tight, so tight.

Heavy rain raps the glass. In the squall there are footsteps, somebody running, somebody whose shoes scuff the gravel. And a drumming, lightly-strummed discord—G, D, F sharp, B flat—with the highest note sliding almost imperceptibly by further quarter-tones, the hollow sound becoming an almost echo before fading, fading into sleep.